D1625410

'TIL IT'S GONE

'TIL IT'S GONE

DWAYNE S. JOSEPH

www.urbanbooks.net

Urban Books
1199 Straight Path
West Babylon, NY 11704

ISBN-13: 978-1-60162-062-0
ISBN-10: 1-60162-062-4

First Printing August 2008
Printed in the United States of America

10 9 8 7 6 5 4 3 2 1

*This is a work of fiction. Any references or similarities to ac-
tual events, real people, living, or dead, or to real locales are
intended to give the novel a sense of reality. Any similarity in
other names, characters, places, and incidents is entirely coin-
cidental.*

Distributed by Kensington Publishing Corp.
Submit Wholesale Order to:
Kensington Publishing Corp.
C/O Penguin Group (USA) Inc.
Attention: Order Processing
405 Murray Hill Parkway
East Rutherford, NJ 07073-2316
Phone: 1-800-526-0275
Fax: 1-800-227-9604

Acknowledgments

Thank you God for life.

Wendy, Tatiana, Natalia, Xavier for your love and support. My friends and family for being there. Love you guys. Aleah. . . . keep reading!

To all of the book clubs and readers. Your feedback, emails and reviews truly mean everything to me. From the bottom of my heart, my goal is to keep you all flipping those pages! Thank you for supporting my effort!! Please continue to hit me up on myspace and please continue to post those reviews.

Read and enjoy . . . But get ready for Home Wrecker. I'm about to SHUT THINGS DOWN!

Thanks to Urban Books for doing what you do. Nicole Peters . . . will you get your feet off the desk and do something! Lol Portia for your friendship and support. La Jill and Eric Pete for being family. Peron Long . . . it's going to be a whole lot of fun!

To my New York Giants!!!!!!SUPER BOWL BABY!!!!!!!!!!!!!!
We wanted it more!!!!! 18&1 . . . Write that down!

Peace!

Dwayne S. Joseph
www.myspace.com/dwaynesjoseph
Djoseph21044@yahoo.com

Dedicated to love's lost and found

PROLOGUE

11:00 PM

Diary,

Today marked a new chapter in my so-called life. I saw Jeff today for a few minutes. We couldn't stay together too long because Stephen's parents were having a New Year's get-together. I told Stephen I had an errand to run and then met Jeff at the office. I know what I was doing was wrong. God, I should have never agreed to meet him. But I just couldn't stop myself.

Why is this so hard for me?

Realistically, there is no future with Jeff. Besides, I have a good man in Stephen, despite the rough times we've been having the past six months. This should be a no-brainer for me. I should be putting my focus on fixing my problems with Stephen, not playing second fiddle to a married man with three kids. Doing the right thing should not be hard, but damn it if Jeff didn't stoke a fire in me that's been slowly burning out. But still . . . I shouldn't be ig-noring the right answers. I shouldn't be continuing down a path that will only lead to nowhere.

Diary . . . what am I going to do?

1

Danita Evans

I was in love with two men.

Well . . . in love with one and falling for another.

I didn't plan on it happening. It just did. My grandmother once said that life is one big unpredictable canvas that keeps getting paint applied to it from the day we're born, 'till the day we take our forever sleep. I believe her, but I figured the majority of the picture on my canvas was done once Stephen came along.

We'd been dating for over three years. Three years filled with the usual highs and lows that come with any relationship. I met him through my best friend, Latrice, who'd pretty much made finding me a man her mission after my last debacle of a relationship. She couldn't stand my taste in men, and quite frankly, neither could I. For some reason, I seemed to gravitate to men who pretended to have it going on, only to reveal their true nature in time as lazy, lying, cheating, insecure assholes. I don't know why I chose that type of man. It wasn't like I tried to. I mean, I tried to keep my standards high. I tried to go with the men that seemed to have a good job, their own home—or at least apartment. I tried to stay away from the mama's boys and thugs, although I did like a little ruggedness.

I'd been fighting Latrice's matchmaking desire for over a year, but after my last relationship, I gave in and agreed to go out with Stephen, who'd she been swearing by for months.

"Trust me 'Nita . . . you won't be sorry." Latrice sipped on her Coke and took a bite of her whopper. We were at Burger King meeting for lunch. She wiped the corner of her mouth with a napkin and then continued. "Stephen is the kind of man you need to be with, girl. He's hella-fine, he's got the job, he's got the car, and he's got his own place. No kids, so no baby mama drama. He's never been in the penal system. Girl, I promise you'll be kicking yourself for not agreeing to go out with him sooner. Oh . . . did I mention how fine he was?"

I gave her a look. "If he's got all of the right attributes, 'Trice, why are you trying to hook me up with him and not grab him for yourself?"

Latrice sipped on her Coke again and then shook her head. "I'm taken, girl."

"Whatever," I said with a smirk. "You're taken until the next full wallet comes along."

Latrice gave me the finger.

I gave it back.

She said, "For real, girl, I'm seeing someone. And it's not one of the usual types."

I looked at her skeptically. "Who?"

"Bernard."

I opened my eyes wide. "Bernard? The next-door neighbor from your condo complex?"

"Yes."

"When did this happen?"

"Remember I went out with him a month ago?"

I nodded. "I remember you agreeing to go out just to get him off of your back."

Latrice gave a wicked smile. "Well, he's really good from the back."

I opened my eyes wide. "No way! Are you serious?"

"Yes."

"Bernard? The sweet guy with the simple job?"

"Yes, that Bernard."

"The world is truly coming to an end," I said.

Latrice gave me the finger again. "Shut up."

I laughed.

I first met Latrice in a step aerobics class ten years ago at the gym. I had just moved from Brooklyn, New York to Columbia, Maryland because of a job transfer. Latrice was born and raised in Baltimore, but moved to the suburbs of Columbia to get away from the craziness in the city. I'm a workout junkie, and when I moved, finding a gym was the first thing I did after getting my apartment squared away.

We were both huffing and puffing our way through the class when she looked over at me and out of the blue said, "You wanna get some ice cream?"

Our friendship took off from there. Latrice is a big sister with an ass that makes Vida Guerra's famous rear end look small with her wide child-rearing hips. I'm the complete opposite. I'm petite with hips and have a smaller, rounder apple bottom.

Latrice has no shame in her game. She tells it like it is, and that's what I like about her. We're alike in a lot of ways, except one: our choice of men. We're complete opposites in that area. I may fail, but I try to find a decent man with husband material. Latrice on the other hand . . . The only criterion required for the men she deals with is the size of their wallet. If a brother has bling and pays her some attention, then it's all systems go. Pretty much everyone sees her as being a real shallow bitch. But I know better. Even though she has never admitted it and never would, I think she has low self-esteem because of her size. It's not that she's shallow, but rather the men she deals with are. They see her ass and D cups and give her all the attention in the world. They have no intention of developing anything with her, and Latrice knows that. But I can see in her eyes that because she's a big girl, she doesn't think a legitimate man would give her the time of day. So instead of struggle with trying to find one and to avoid from spending too many nights alone, she goes for the easy target.

I wish she would think higher of herself and leave herself open for that special man, because she's one of the realest sisters I know. Her parents are from Guyana, so she has that whole exotic-look thing going on. She's got dark-chocolate skin, feline-shaped brown eyes that she covers with light green contacts, and a round face with high cheekbones. Her best feature, her smile, could brighten the darkest room. She truly is a beautiful sister. She just happens to be a plus-sized woman. I've tried to talk to her about the men she dates, but she quickly changes the subject. To hear her say that she's into Bernard is shocking, because he's so unlike any man she'd dealt with before.

"I'm in shock, 'Trice."

"Believe me, so am I. I never expected to fall for him, but . . ." She raised her eyebrows and smiled.

I said, "Wow."

"So anyway, that's one reason I didn't try to snag Stephen."

"One reason? There's another?"

"Yes."

"And what's that?"

"He likes his sisters on the lighter shade of caramel, skinny, and with no ass. Well, in your case, a little ass."

My turn to give the finger. "I have an ass, thank you very much. And I'm definitely not skinny."

"But you are on the lighter side of the fence."

"So he's one of those types?"

"No girl. He's cool. For real. I know him. He's a real brother. Only likes sisters. He just likes 'em light, that's all."

"And skinny."

"That too."

"Guess we won't go any further than the one date then, huh?"

"You're gonna like him, girl."

"You said that about Leonard too."

Leonard Biggs. Months prior, I was going to give in and go out with Leonard, a guy from her job. But fortunately, I saw him before the actual date had been set up.

"Leonard was a nice guy."

"Nice didn't make up for how ugly his ass was. How could you have even attempted to set me up with him? I'm supposed to be your girl."

"I was tired of the knuckleheads you kept choosing. I just figured Leonard would be a nice change of pace."

"You know you were wrong for that, right?"

Latrice laughed.

"And you swear Stephen is no Leonard."

"Sheeit. Far from it, Danita. The man could model if he wanted to."

I humph'd.

Latrice said, "You'll see."

I raised my eyebrows and sighed. "I guess I will."

We finished off our lunch and then grabbed our purses to head back to our jobs. I was a manager for the Limited in the mall. Like Stephen, Latrice was also a project manager at E-Systems.

Before leaving for her car, I said, "What time should I expect him?"

Latrice said, "He'll be by your house at seven-thirty to pick you up. Try to be ready, because he is never late. And wear that short black skirt you have. Show him those legs you be stepping for."

That night, I wore the skirt and a white sleeveless top. I figured if I was going to go through with the date, I'd better make damn sure I looked the part. I wore my Victoria's Secret's Very Sexy for Her perfume as an added bonus.

When Stephen rang my bell at exactly 7:30, I paused with my hand on the doorknob and whispered, " 'Trice, if he ain't fine . . ." Then I opened the door.

I have to admit that Latrice was on point when she described his looks. He was a fine dark-skinned brother with light brown bedroom eyes, soft lips, and a button nose so cute—it was too cute. I couldn't complain at all. I took a quick minute to check out his lean frame. He wore a form-fitting black cotton top with black slacks. And dangling from his neck was a simple silver cross. Nothing too gaudy. I liked that. I also liked the size of his arms and chest. I could tell that he worked out.

From the rise of his eyebrows and his struggle to keep his eyes from going up and down on me, he approved of what he saw as well.

He extended his hand. "Hello, Danita."

I took his hand. His fingers were damp and clammy. Good, at least I wasn't the only one who was nervous. "Hello, Stephen."

"Ready to go?"

"Absolutely."

We went to the Rusty Scupper by the harbor in Baltimore, and sat by the window, ate seafood, and talked for hours while an old gentleman played love songs on the piano. Stephen fascinated me from the moment he opened his mouth. Not only was he attractive, with a set of eyelashes to die for, but he was intelligent too. He truly seemed genuine and that made him all the more attractive.

As the date went on, we found we had a lot in common. We were both fans of the NFL, though we cheered for different teams. He was crazy about the Baltimore Ravens, while I was a die-hard New York Giants fan, thanks to my father. We both loved jazz and going to the movies. Our political views were the same, although he liked Obama while I preferred Hillary.

As the night went on, and the more we talked and became more comfortable around one another, I decided to test the waters and see where his head was.

"I hear you don't date dark-skinned women. What's up with that?" I looked at him with my best accusatory black-woman glare and waited eagerly for his response.

He shook his head. "I have nothing against darker-skinned women. I hope Latrice didn't tell you that."

"Have you ever dated a dark-skinned sister?"

"A few, actually."

I gave him a playful scowl. "Mmm-hmm."

"A woman's skin color really means nothing to me. Now I won't lie . . . even though it's not a conscious thing for me, I have dated more light-skinned sisters."

"Mmm-hmm."

"Honestly, if a woman is beautiful, she's beautiful no matter what shade or race."

"I see." That was a good answer.

"Just being real with you."

"Being real is always good."

We talked more until the restaurant closed. After that, we took a silent stroll by the harbor, enjoying the warm night and each other's company. When he took me home, we exchanged numbers and made plans for another date. The date ended with a kiss good night. No tongue, though. Not yet.

Before I went to bed that night, I called Latrice, because if I didn't, I knew she'd be calling me in the middle of the night for details.

"You were right, girl."

"I told you!" Latrice yelled. "Ain't he fine?"

"I'm gonna have to give you your props, 'Trice. He damn sure ain't no Leonard."

"Made your heart jump when you saw him, didn't he!"

"Just fall down and do backflips."

Latrice burst out in laughter.

"Stephen has it going on, girl. He's sexy as sin, and intelligent. I don't see how he can't be taken already."

"He could be now if you want him. Now what did you two do? My eyes are gettin' heavy. Tell me before I fall asleep. Where did you two go that kept you out until two-thirty?"

"Well, *Mama*, he took me to the Rusty Scupper for dinner."

"That place ain't cheap, girl."

"I know. And it was romantic. We had a nice view of the water and talked over candlelight for hours. After that, we just walked the harbor and talked some more. Then he brought me home."

"And?"

"And what?"

"Is he passed out on the bed or the couch?"

I laughed. "You're a fool, girl!"

"What? It's two o'clock in the morning on a Monday night. The good clubs aren't open, and restaurants close after eleven. Don't tell me all you did was walk and talk and then said good night."

"I didn't sleep with him, if that's what you want to know."

"Didn't sleep with him?"

"That's what I said. All we did was talk. We were gettin' to know each other. What more did you expect?"

She sucked her teeth. "A man that fine shouldn't have to wait to get a taste. You need to start takin' advantage of the opportunities as they come."

"Sorry, girl, but some of us just don't do give up the booty on the first date. Besides, he was a true gentleman and didn't even try to push up on me."

"But if he would have . . ."

I smiled. "Maybe I would have given him some," I said, laughing.

"Ha! You ho!"

"Whatever!"

"So . . . are you two going to go out again?"

"Yes. We exchanged numbers, and we're going out this weekend."

"That is just great, Danita!"

"I have to say thank you, Latrice. You really looked out for a sister."

"That's what friends are for, ho!"

"Good night, trick!" I said with a smile.

"Night, girl."

To my surprise, the next date with Stephen came a lot sooner than anticipated. He called me the next day after work and invited me to the movies. We went back to his place afterward and watched the NFL Network.

I never went home that night.

When I tried, we shared a hug. That hug led to a kiss, which led to a little tongue. The next thing I knew, we were in his bed, rearranging his sheets.

It had been awhile since I'd felt a man deep inside of me, and with his thickness and length, I felt just that. Stephen worked me up, down, backward and forward. I took him sideways and in diagonal loops. We made love three times that night. Neither one of us could get enough. We licked, sucked, pulled, nibbled, rode, orgasmed, and sweated our way to lovemaking that you only read about in books or see in the movies.

I didn't give all the details, but I did call Latrice the next day and let her know that I wasn't as slow as she thought I was.

"He has skills, girl. Skills!"

"You didn't?"

"Three times."

"Dayum! You trick. It was that good?"

" 'Trice, he took me downtown, uptown, in town, and then around."

"Dayum, girl. I need to call Bernard right now. You have me all worked up over here."

"You better not open your big mouth and say anything to Stephen at work, Latrice."

"My lips are sealed."

"They better be. I don't want him having the wrong impression of me."

"I think he's fine with the impression he has already."

I saw Stephen almost everyday after that. We spent as much time together as we could, getting to know the ins and outs of each other. He told me about his family—both parents, alive and kicking. One brother, younger by six years, but taller. I told him about mine: one parent, my mama. Father who died when I was thirteen. No brother or sister, but "I had a dog."

The more I saw of Stephen and his curly top, the more I wanted to see him. I clicked with him in a way that I had never done with any man before. He made me laugh with his sense of humor. He made me smile just by smiling himself. For the first time, my choice in men had been the right one.

We moved in together after dating for six months. Actually, I moved in with him. He'd made the suggestion. I took him up on it. Despite the short length of time, the time was right for us to take the next step in our relationship. We both knew we were at the point where we just needed to see if there was such a thing as too much time together. A week after he suggested it, I had my things unpacked in his territory.

In the beginning, we couldn't get enough of each other. We took showers together, ate together, and woke up together—always together. We rarely did anything apart. We even shopped for furniture and redecorated the apartment with a reflection of us. Not just him. Besides, I wasn't really feeling his black contemporary flair. So we chose new, sophisticated furniture. Well, I chose—he just nodded. Before long, we had the dining room decked out with an oak dining set, the living room with a dark-cherry entertainment center and matching center and side tables. We replaced his boring vertical blinds with burgundy drapes and changed the color of the bathroom from blue to a mixture of olive green and cream. In the bedroom, we got rid of the water bed, because it hurt my back, and bought a dark pine bed with rising columns and a matching dresser and night table. Yeah, our place was definitely starting to take on a new, more inviting shape.

Our relationship was all that I had been wanting and more. In Stephen, I found a man who had become my best friend. He was there for me on the best and worst of days. And I, in turn, made sure to let him know he was my king and that I was his queen who would always stand by his side. With every day that passed, our love blossomed. But as always, with every bright day, there's a dark night trailing behind it.

2

Unfortunately, the bad times for Stephen and me came two years into our union. It was a Saturday morning, and he was sleeping in. He had gone out with his best friend Carlos the night before. I'm an early bird by nature and a clean freak on the weekends, so before the clock had struck 8:00, I had already done the bathroom and the living room and was getting ready to wash clothes. Because the cream-colored pants he wore the night before had a red stain on them, I decided to throw them in with a few other things. When a condom fell from the back pocket, I couldn't move.

A condom.

After two years together, Stephen and I didn't use condoms.

I tried not to, but seeing it took me back to a time when I'd found empty condom wrappers stashed in a secret compartment of my ex's Cherokee. Mike—a womanizing son of a bitch, who played the hell out of me. He was a cop, a single father, and I had fallen for him hard. Thought he was as good as he claimed to be. Like I said, he played the hell out of me. Finding the condoms really broke my heart, because I really thought we had something. I saw a future with him. I was actually naive enough to think that he wouldn't dog me the way others before him had. I was wrong. So wrong. After that I built up a wall around my heart and swore to never take it down again.

Once the initial shock wore off, anger set in. I wanted answers.

"What the hell is this?" I yelled, rushing into the bedroom. Stephen didn't move or respond from underneath the covers. I shook him hard and in a voice ten times louder than before, said, "Stephen . . . Why do you have a condom in your pocket? What ho are you fucking?" I was boiling. Felt like two hundred degrees beneath my skin, and getting hotter by the second.

Stephen stirred and pulled the cover away from his head. He looked at me through half-closed eyes. "Danita, what the hell?"

I tapped my foot on the ground furiously. "Don't *what the hell* me, ass! Who are you fucking?"

"Who am I fucking? What are you talking about?"

I threw the condom at him. "This fell out of your pocket, asshole! The one you wore last night when you went out."

Stephen groaned and grabbed the condom. Looking at it, he shook his head. As he did, he had the nerve to crack a smile.

"What the hell are you smiling about? I don't see anything amusing about this."

"Danita, calm down. I can explain."

"Yeah . . . you better. And it better be a damn good explanation."

Stephen stretched and yawned. His cavalier attitude only made me angrier.

"Danita, that's not mine."

"Oh really? Then who the hell's is it? Or are the pants you came home in not yours either?"

Stephen stared back at me through his sleepy eyes. His smile was gone. "Damn, Danita, will you just calm down. The condom belongs to Carlos. He left it in my car."

"How convenient for you."

"It fell out of his pocket."

"And landed in yours, huh? What, were you unlucky in your quest for ass last night? Is that why you still have it? Or was this an extra one that you didn't get to use?"

Stephen sat up in the bed. "Are you accusing me of sleeping around on you?"

"Are you?"

"You can't be serious."

"You didn't answer the question."

"I don't need to answer the question!"

I wagged my finger and shook my head. "I know you are not raising your voice at me like that. I'm not the one that came home at three in the morning with a condom that *we* certainly don't use. Talking about it's Carlos's." I sucked my teeth. "Please. I'm not some naive bitch."

Stephen groaned. "Do you want me to call Carlos so you can talk to him and get your fucking answers?"

I sucked my teeth again. "Right. Let's do that, because he most certainly wouldn't have your back."

Stephen let out a curse and then lay back against the headboard. I stared at him with venom as my mind went back to Mike. My heart was beating heavily, like drums being pounded on out of frustration. I looked at the condom that he still held in his hand. I imagined him opening it, taking it out of the wrapper, and sliding down his shaft. Saw him fucking another bitch.

I folded my arms across my chest. "So?"

"So what, Danita? I gave you the answer you wanted."

"The answer I wanted? What about the truth?"

"That was the goddamned truth! Shit! This is ridiculous."

"Ridiculous? How would you like it if you found a condom in my purse, ass! How would you take it if I told you it was Latrice's?"

"I'm not lying, Danita!"

"The hell you aren't!" I yelled. Both he and Mike were in my head now. Both of them laughing at me.

Tears were welling in the bottom of my eyes, threatening to cascade down my cheeks. I couldn't believe that we were having this argument. I couldn't believe I had found that condom. I fell for it once. Swore to never fall again. Of all men . . . Stephen. I couldn't believe it. Didn't want to believe it.

"Goddamn, Danita!" Stephen yelled, getting up from the bed. "I can't believe you're tripping like this."

"Tripping?"

"Yes! Shit! Asking me if I'm sleeping around. Come on. You know me. You know what I'm about. How are you even gonna accuse me of doing that to you?"

I glared at him for a long, pregnant second. Thought about Mike and how he'd dogged me again. He wasn't the first, but he was definitely the worst. I wanted to believe Stephen. I really did. "Carlos's huh?"

Stephen nodded. "Yes. Carlos's."

"Couldn't you come up with a better excuse than that?"

Stephen put his hands on his sides and dropped his chin to his chest and shook his head. "This is bullshit, Danita and you know it." He looked up at me. "You know me."

I slit my eyes. "Do I?"

He clenched his jaws and then said, "You're kidding me, right? You're not really overblowing this, right?"

"Overblowing? Nigga, a condom fell out of your pocket and you give me the it's-a-friend's line?"

"Jesus Christ, Danita!" Stephen yelled. "This is unbelievable!" He moved past me and went to the closet and slid into a pair of sweats and T-shirt.

"Where the fuck are you going? We're not finished."

"Danita . . . I'm finished. You can stay and argue all you want." Without another word, he grabbed his keys from the dresser and walked out of the room.

Things started to change after that. Little by little, the wall that he had broken down started to form again. I felt like I had to watch my back. I really wanted to believe him, but I was scared to. I know it was all in my head, but my imagination was driving me insane. When Stephen said he was going to the store, I pictured him running off to a rendezvous with some silly bitch. When he came home from the gym and showered, I wondered whether he was sweaty from the workout or sex. When he was on his cell, I wondered about the person on the other end. I couldn't get thoughts like that to leave me alone. They ate away at me on a day-to-day basis. I questioned him, called him constantly, and insisted I go places with him, all because I didn't trust him.

Of course my lack of trust pissed him off and we would go at it. Day by day, things got worse between us. We stopped talking, stopped being intimate, practically stopped being friends.

The strong bond that we had was ripping apart at the seams, all because of that fucking ribbed-for-extra-pleasure condom.

3

It wasn't just my relationship with Stephen that was leading the way toward a breakdown. I felt like everything in my life was crumbling. My job in the mall was wearing me out. My relationship with my mama was stressing me out too because she loved Stephen. She wanted him to be her son-in-law, and would probably have adopted him if she could. So as our problems increased, it only got on my nerves when I would visit her and she'd want to know where Stephen was.

"You never come over here without him, but you have the last few times. What's going on with you two?"

"We just have some issues, Mama, that's all."

"Issues? Issues like what?"

"Just issues, Mama."

"Danita, Rome wasn't built in a day, you know. All relationships have their good and bad moments. It takes work."

"Yeah . . . too much work," I said, fiddling with

the cup of tea I was drinking as we sat at her kitchen table.

"Do you love him, Danita?"

I nodded my head as tears welled. "Yes, Mama."

"Then it's never too much work. Listen, baby, if there's one thing I can tell you, it's to never let a good man go to waste. And baby, Stephen is a good man. And he loves you."

Tears falling freely now, I said "I know, Mama. It's just . . . I found a condom in his pocket, and when . . . when I asked him about it, he said it belonged to Carlos."

"Okay, and what's the problem?"

I looked up at her. "The problem? He had a condom."

"And he told you who it belonged to."

"And I'm supposed to believe him?"

"Yes, baby. Yes, you are."

I paused, going back to that day.

"Mama . . . I've been down this road before."

"Stephen is no Mike, Danita. You really have to let that go."

"Mike wasn't the only one, Mama. He was the worst, but not the only."

"Again, Stephen is not Mike, or any other men you've dealt with."

"So I'm just supposed to take his word?"

"Yes!"

"And when I wind up being the fool again, then what!" I said, louder than I intended.

My mother gave me a watch-your-tone-with-me look. "How do you know you are going to be played for a fool, Danita? Do you have a crystal ball?"

"No, but—"

"But nothing! Are you really going to risk losing

a good man because you can't get past a jerk from your past?"

"Jerks, Mama. Plural!"

"I've dealt with jerks before, Danita. And it wasn't always sunshine and flowers for your father and me either. Yes, some problems are worse than others, but when you love someone, and it's real, you make it work. He's a good man, Danita. What you two have is real and good."

"How do you know, Mama? How do you know?"

"Because I can see the magic in you two. I can see it because your father and I had it. I'm telling you, don't let the past ruin what could be a very good future."

I shook my head and wiped tears away. I heard her words, knew they were sound, knew the advice she was giving was the best, but my fear just wouldn't let me accept them. I pushed the mug away from me and stood up. "I have to go, Mama."

I swear if it wasn't one thing, it was another. My job definitely had a lot to do with my unhappiness also. I was underpaid, overworked, and I had to deal with a lot of bullshit on a daily basis, and with the firing of our district manager, I had picked up double duty without so much as a thank-you or a raise. I was tired of working my ass off for pennies when I knew I could do something else and make some dimes.

Without Stephen to turn to, I could only turn to my girl, who, over lunch one day, just let me rant and rave without interruption.

When I was finished, Latrice said, "Feel better?"

I shook my head. "No. Well, just a little. Thank you."

"Girl, if you hate your job so much, why don't you just quit?"

I sighed. "And do what, 'Trice? I didn't finish college, and I don't know much about computers aside from being able to buy things online, send e-mails, and do Google searches. As much as I hate to admit it, I have limited skills."

"Girl, college is overrated and expensive, and I know you know how to use Excel, Access, and Word, so you have skills. Look at me. I went to school for biology and look at what I'm doing."

"You have a good job, Latrice."

"Yeah, in a field I knew nothing about."

"Your degree helped you get your foot in the door, though."

Latrice raised her eyebrows. "No. What helped me get in the door was because my daddy went to school with my manager. Not what you know, girl."

"I know. It's who you know that matters."

" 'Nita, listen . . . you know I didn't know shit about telecommunications or managing projects. I was lucky, girl. That's all. If my daddy hadn't gone to school with my boss, I might be flipping burgers somewhere."

"Whatever."

"Okay . . . maybe sliding up and down a pole, then."

We both laughed.

"For real, girl, unless I went for my master's or doctorate, I wouldn't be doing much with my bio degree. Believe me, if I can get lucky like that, you can too."

"Not all of us have hookups like that."

"Want me to put a word in at work?"

"Hell no! It's bad enough seeing Stephen at home right now."

"So his story about the condom is still the same?"

"Hasn't altered in the slightest."

"You ever think he could be telling you the truth?"

"A friend, Latrice. He said the condom was a friend's. And not just any friend, but Carlos. And you know how Carlos likes to roll."

"I do. But Stephen isn't Carlos."

"Look, I had this conversation with my mother already. Can we please not discuss this right now? I'm dealing with this the best way I know how."

"I know, girl. I just don't like to see you guys fighting like this. Especially if it could be over nothing."

"Over nothing? Let me ask you something. What would you have done if you had found the condom in Bernard's pocket?"

"Sheeeeeit!"

"My point exactly."

Latrice held up her hand. She was wearing several gold bracelets that jingled as she spoke. "Hold up now. You never let me finish."

"Oh by all means, please do."

"Now, if that had been Bernard, and I had found a condom in his pocket, which I know better never happen, I would ask him about it."

"And when he said it was a friend's?"

"I'd curse his ass out."

"All right, then."

Latrice shook her head. "Girl, I honestly don't know what I would've done."

"All right, then."

"But I will say this . . . knowing Bernard the way I do, I would let it go."

"Are you sure about that?"

" 'Nita, it's either that or lose my man. You just have to be secure enough in yourself, your man, and the relationship. The question is . . . are you?"

I didn't answer because I didn't know.

Latrice raised an eyebrow. "Look girl, you heard his explanation, and you still decided to keep the relationship going. You need to stand by that decision and let the past be just that. Focus on the now. Besides, Stephen is a good man who loves you and has been there for you like no other man before him has ever been. Really . . . why not just believe him?"

"Easier said than done."

"Never said it was."

We switched topics and started commenting on the men walking around in the mall, who were either looking broke as a joke, or finer than wine, when Latrice suddenly slammed her palm on the table. "I may have a hookup."

"I told you I don't want to work with Stephen. Besides, I don't know the first thing about what you do."

"Not at my job, girl. A friend of mine works at a law firm. She's a paralegal there. She told me the other day that her boss is going to be looking for a new receptionist. Job pays eighteen an hour."

My eyes lit up. "Really? Hook a sister up, would you?"

She did, and the next week I had an interview at Beers and Grimes law firm. That hookup changed my life for good.

That's when I met Jeff.

12:00 AM

Diary,
 Sorry I haven't written in so long. I've been busy at work and home.

I got a nice surprise today—Jeff came back from vacation with his family a day early. I was thrilled to see him when he walked into work this morning. I have to admit, ever since he left, I couldn't get him off my mind. I kept thinking about the last time that we saw each other, just hours before he had left for vacation. We waited until everyone left the office, and then shared a few tender kisses and hugs. I like the way he kisses. He takes his time. He's not all over the place with his tongue. Stephen's a great kisser too, but with Stephen, there's no romance. Jeff's are filled with it. He kisses like he wants me to enjoy it more than he does. He's that way with everything. He's always concerned about my wants. It's nice being satisfied free of charge.

Before he left, he gave me a dozen red roses. They were beautiful. I kissed him and then put them in a vase and put them on my desk at work. When anyone asked, I said they were from Stephen.

I felt a release when he came back to work. Felt like I could breathe and do my job comfortably again. I hated to see him go in the first place, but I know he has his family to take care of. That's the only thing about our arrangement that I hate. I have to be fifth in line for his attention and time. His wife is first, then his three kids. I know I'm wrong to feel jealous of them, but it's hard not to. I used to feel that way with Stephen. I used to want to be with him all of the time, but time and our unresolved issues have changed all of that. Sometimes I wonder if that feeling of wanting to be with Stephen will ever come back. He was my life at one point, before the condom. Before the excuse and the arguments. I'm not so sure about what I want now. But Jeff is. He says he wants me. He says I make him wild with passion. Can you believe that? If he only knew what he did to me.

Jeff and I listened to soft jazz while we cuddled on the floor in his office. We didn't say a word. We just lay there and soaked in each other's essence. Like Stephen, he's a gentle man. Loves to caress in all the right places, in all the right ways. We still haven't slept together yet. I'm not emotionally ready, although my body is. Thankfully, Jeff doesn't pressure me, but he does push the issue with his caresses and kisses.

I have made love to Jeff in my dreams, though. There, Jeff and I take each other to heights of ecstasy that leave me wet and needing a shower. My dreams make me think of a song that the group Shai sings—"Mr. Turn U Out." Actually, the first few lines of the song are what gets to me. That's where Mr. Turn U Out speaks.

Jeff is my fantasy. My Mr. Turn U Out. Only he's very real. And he has my emotions in a stranglehold.

Before we parted and went back to our separate lives, we made plans to have one of our "lunches" tomorrow. We'd been doing that a lot lately. Having lunch sometimes at a restaurant somewhere where no one would recognize us. I don't know where we're going with this relationship we have. It would be nice, but I don't expect him to leave his wife and kids for me. Sometimes, that can be a bitter pill to swallow.

If my mama knew what I was doing, she'd have a heart attack and then probably disown me. But I can't really worry about that. I need to be happy. My mama wouldn't understand that. I know Stephen's a good man, but even good men lie. It's *not that my love for Stephen has completely gone. He's still very special to me. He has all of the qualities any woman would require in her significant other. But again, that damn condom. Some days I've tried to let the past go. Tried to overcome the bitter memories. But is it too late now? I mean, even if I did accept his answer for what it is, with Jeff in the picture, would it change anything at this point? Why did God bring Jeff into my life?*

The other night when I got home, Stephen had a candlelight dinner made out for me. He wanted to talk about us. He wanted us to be close again. It almost brought me to tears to see the sincerity in his brown eyes. I love him. I really do. I love his smile, his companionship. We've invested so much time in us, and it's almost hard imagining giving that up. But again . . . it all goes back to the condom. I ask myself so many times why I continue to stay with him if I'm not completely happy. If I can't let my past go, why hold on? Even with the issues, am I just too used to him being around? What would I do if he was no longer a part of my life? Sometimes, I'm scared to know the answer.

4

Jeff Beers.

The other man in my life. Twelve years my senior. And my boss. Of all the people in the world, this had to happen to me.

The day of the interview was the first time we met. It was fall—October. I wore a pair of gray slacks with heels and a form-fitting white button-down dress shirt. I was conservatively sexy.

When Latrice first told me about the opportunity, I assumed that Beers and Grimes was a white firm. I was shocked when I walked into the office and saw that was not the case. The atmosphere was quiet and all business. A nice change from what I had been used to at the mall. The professional atmosphere put an immediate smile on my face. People were there to work and not profile.

I was greeted by Latrice's friend when I walked in. "You must be Danita," she said with a smile. "I'm Emily." She was an average-height, attractive white female with light freckles on her cheeks and

the tip of her nose. She couldn't have been any
more than twenty-one.

I shook her hand. "Thank you for putting the
word in," I said quietly.

"It was nothing, girl. We needed somebody bad,
and Latrice said you were the right person for the
job."

"How long have you known 'Trice?"

"I met her just a few months ago. We met at a
toy party of a mutual friend."

"Oh, that must have been Regina," I said with a
smile. "I was supposed to go, but I had to work that
night."

"It's a shame you weren't there. You could've
been working here sooner."

I smiled. I liked her. I see why Latrice did too.
"Destiny has a funny way of working sometimes."

"Very true. Well listen, I have to get back to
work. I just wanted to come and meet you and let
you know that you're in already. The interview is
just a formality. Jeff and Will trust my judgment,
and I trust Latrice's. So, welcome aboard."

"When they give me a starting date, I'll come
over and thank you," I said with a genuine smile.
That was my way of saying that nothing was guar-
anteed until it happened. She smiled again and
nodded her head.

I sat in the waiting area for a good twenty minutes before one of the partners came out and
greeted me with an outstretched hand. "Ms. Evans,
how do you do? I'm William Grimes, but you can
call me Will."

I took his very large hand and smiled. "Nice to
meet you, Mr. Grimes," I said, letting him know
that I wasn't comfortable with the first-name basis

yet. He flashed a handsome smile, exposing perfect, but dim, yellow teeth, from smoking no doubt. He was tall, about six feet seven, with gray speckles in a neatly shaped Afro. The suit he had on looked tailored. He wasn't the most attractive man. His eyes were beady and too close together, his nose was broad and looked like it had been broken in the past, and his skin was leathery from the smoking. He looked to be in his fifties. Not the most handsome, but his smile compensated for that.

"Sorry to have kept you waiting so long. It's been a crazy day here."

"The wait was nothing at all."

He smiled again. "Well . . . follow me. My partner, Jeff, will be joining us soon. We've both heard good things about you."

"I'm glad." And I was. I made a mental note to invite Emily out to lunch—my treat.

We went to the back and sat in a conference room with expensive cherrywood furniture. Against the walls were cherrywood bookcases filled with law books from A to Z. I sat on the right side of the table, in a comfortable dark brown leather chair. Before William sat down, he moved to a coffee machine sitting by the far wall. "Would you like a cup of coffee, Ms. Evans?"

"I'm a tea drinker, and no thank you. But I appreciate the offer."

William poured some coffee and threw in a few packets of sugar and then sat down across from me. "I used to be a tea drinker until I started working until two and three in the morning."

"Wow."

"Yeah, tell me about it. Once I started doing that, I had to drink coffee to keep myself awake and alert. It's not good for a lawyer to be falling asleep in the middle of a cross-examination."

I laughed. "No. That might hurt your credibility just a little."

"Not to mention my client's chances!"

We both laughed and as we were, Jeff sauntered inside, looking like anything but a lawyer in a pair of khaki pants, brown sandals, and a white linen top. Covering his eyes were a pair of tinted shades. He wasn't as tall as William, but he was bulkier. Probably went to the gym a few times a week. He was devilishly handsome, but still, at that time, I didn't think too highly of him because, unlike Will, he had an I-think-I'm-the-shit attitude, which was a turnoff.

Especially after my ex, Mike, men who perpetrated as though they were all that, when they were actually nothing at all, really irked me. Besides, this was supposed to be an interview. If I had to look my best, I would've at least expected the same from them. But then again, I was the one who needed the job.

"What's up, Will?" he said, nodding at his partner. He didn't even acknowledge me until after he had gotten a cup of coffee and sat down. He removed his shades and extended his hand. "How do you do, Danita?"

Danita? When did I tell him to use my first name?

"Just fine, Mr. Beers," I said, shaking his hand and giving him the same message that I had given his partner.

"That's good. Beautiful day out, isn't it?"

"If you like the fall, I suppose." His nonchalance was annoying.

"You don't like the fall?"

I tried again. "I'm a summer person, Mr. Beers. I like the heat and the sunshine."

He either didn't catch where I was coming from, or didn't care.

"I'm a fall guy all the way. Love the fall. Love the colors of the leaves as they change from green to red, to red-yellow, to brown. Love the breeze that flows. You and Will can have the heat and humidity."

I smiled to be nice and then looked from him to his partner. They were complete opposites. William was pristine in his black suit and yellow tie, while Jeff looked like a man refusing to accept the fact that he was no longer a teenager. It was hard to imagine them being partners. We sat with smiles on our faces, until Jeff asked, "So when can you start, Danita?"

"How soon do you need me to start?"

Jeff looked at me with a smile that was just slightly alluring. "Well, since you're here and obviously dressed for the part, how about today?"

Both William and I raised our eyebrows in surprise. It was obvious to me who the lead dog had been. I hadn't told my job about my interview. No need to let them know I was on the hunt. The thought of leaving my job without notice didn't sit too well with me. I never liked to burn my bridges.

"I really should give my other job two weeks' notice."

"The job pays twenty-two an hour," Jeff said.

Again, William and I raised eyebrows.

Twenty-two an hour. Four dollars more than what Latrice had said. A hell of a raise from the twelve I was making at the mall.

Two tears in a bucket.

"Where do I sit? And what do I do?"

Jeff smiled that almost titillating smile and stood up. "Welcome to the team," he said, extending his hand.

I took it, but when I had tried to pull away, very subtly, he wouldn't let go. We locked eyes for a brief second. He spoke to me without words. Before the interview maybe I would have been a bit more responsive, but he was a stranger then. Now he was my boss. I pulled my hand away.

"Well," he said, moving away from the table. "I wish I could chat with you longer, but I have things to do, people to sue." He laughed and headed toward the door. "Enjoy your first day here, Danita."

"Thank you, Mr. Beers."

"Oh, and one more thing, Danita. Around here, we're all business, but we're all on a first-name basis. Please use mine, as I will be using yours." Without another word, he left the room.

I looked at William. He seemed to be deep in thought. I wondered if it was because he had just been treated like an employee rather than an equal.

"Ready whenever you are," I said.

I called the job later to let them know that I wouldn't be coming back. Before I sat down at my very own desk, I thanked Emily.

5

It took awhile for anything to develop between Jeff and me. For the first few months, we were all business. I answered the phone calls for the firm, took messages for the lawyers and paralegals, and typed up standard letters pertaining to individual cases. Although I missed some of my coworkers from the store, my new coworkers had their own identity that I really enjoyed.

There were two whites in the office. Henry, a nice guy, short, with thinning hair and glasses as thick as Coke bottles. He was another lawyer, who seemed to work on a part-time basis. He was funny and a great conversationalist. If you were down, make no mistake, Henry could pick you up.

The other white, Emily, and I grew closer as we worked together. She was a paralegal and started coming to lunch with Latrice and me. She was cool peoples, for a white girl. To be honest, she had more attitude than some black women I knew, and she had a thing for the brothers. I think her skin was supposed to have been a shade or two darker.

Then there was Rodney, an ugly brother with an even uglier smile and attitude. He was bald, tall, skinny, and had frightened eyes. I didn't know how he managed to end up with his wife, who could've easily been a model. I guess his salary had made him one hell of a good-looking man. He and I didn't get along too well. I didn't like him or the way he blatantly stared at my ass. He didn't like me either, because I never kissed his ass. I usually took care of anything he needed last, which pissed him off.

Next was Tanya. She was the elder of the crew. She was a paralegal who'd been with the firm for over six years. Short and pudgy, she walked around with an infectious smile all day long. She usually kept to herself. The others called her antisocial and stuck-up because she didn't really interact with anyone. Having been there as long as she had, I figured she was smart by being the way she was. I'm sure she avoided a lot of drama that way.

Finally, there was Renea and Jai. It took awhile for me to get to know them because they didn't really deal with anyone else but each other. Rumor was they were lesbian lovers. But the way Jai talked and acted, you wouldn't have known it. Jai was tall and attractive. Her background was black, Italian, and Spanish. She had long hair, dark olive-toned skin, and green eyes. With her slim frame and big breasts, the men in and out of the office drooled over her and the short skirts she loved to wear, and her low-cut tops that showed off her cleavage. If she was a lesbian, she definitely hadn't been ready to come out of the closet.

If they were lovers, Renea was most definitely the man to Jai's woman. On the butch side, with a low Afro and manly features, she was thick-boned with more muscle than any of the men in the office. Her dark brown eyes were always laced with evil intent. Basically, she always looked like she was mad at the world.

Like I said, the first few months were all business for me. I dealt with Jeff and Will only when I had to. Neither one of them were there much. They were always out meeting potential clients or in court. When they were in, I didn't see them much then either, because they were always tucked away in their offices. Will was the quiet partner, who always had a smile on his face. He never really said much. He just made sure that everyone was doing what he or she was supposed to have been doing. He handled most of the finances for the firm. He also signed the paychecks. He and I got along well.

Jeff, on the other hand . . .

In the beginning, we used to bump heads frequently. At one point, I didn't think I was going to last too long there. His cocky and abrasive attitude worked my first, second, and last nerve. He thought he was the shit, always coming in with casual clothing and sneakers. He certainly didn't fit the stereotype of a lawyer the way Will had. It amazed me that he was a father and husband, as much as he flirted with Jai and Emily. He rarely spoke to me when he saw me. Probably thought I was a bitch, which was all right with me, because I didn't want to be flirted with.

That's why it surprised me one day when, after everyone had gone for the day, he approached me and asked me out to dinner. I had been working late, trying to get some things done that I couldn't do because the phones hadn't stopped ringing that day, when he asked. I stopped with what I was doing and looked at him.

"Excuse me?"

He gave me that same smile he had given me during my interview months before. "I asked if you'd like to go out to dinner."

I curled my lips. Just like a dog, I thought. "Aren't you married with kids?"

He laughed. Damn, I had to admit it was sexy. "Yes, I am. Nice to see you remembered. All I'm asking for is dinner. I'd like to discuss some things with you."

"Oh, so this is a *business* dinner then?"

"Where we'll discuss business. Exactly."

"And we can't discuss that here? My dinners are usually reserved for my man," I lied. Stephen and I hadn't had dinner together for a while. Things were really strained between us, but no need for anyone else, least of all my boss, to know that.

He looked at my framed picture of Stephen on my desk. "I see. Well, sometimes, I like to get away from the office. What does your man do?"

"He's a project manager."

Jeff nodded. "So how about dinner?"

I closed my eyes a bit. "This is kind of random, isn't it? I mean, you barely speak a word to me during the day. And now you're coming out of nowhere and asking me to dinner?"

"To discuss business, yes. And I rarely have time for talking during the day."

"You seem to make time to talk to Emily and Jai."

Jeff looked at me and flashed a subtle smile. He seemed to be enjoying my standoffish demeanor. "I've known Emily and Jai a lot longer than you. Stick around and we'll be talking just as much."

I said *umm-hmm* with my eyes.

Jeff smiled, and for the first time, I noticed how attractive his eyes had been. They were somewhat sleepy, sort of like Marvin Gaye's, and a light shade of gray. He said, "So . . . dinner?"

"Again, my dinners are reserved."

"How about Thursday?"

I pulled my head back a bit. Had he not heard what I'd said? "Jeff—"

"Danita, I spend the majority of my time in this office. Too much time, actually. Since your hire date, neither myself nor Will have gotten to meet with you to see how things are going. Usually, I'd like to do that for lunch, but as both of our schedules have become increasingly more hectic, dinner is the best time in which to touch base with you. So . . . how is Thursday?"

I wanted to put up a fight, but I couldn't argue with what he'd said. I hadn't met with either of them and their days had left little time for any type of real conversation. And I admit, I was curious to know what they thought of my work so far.

I nodded my head. "Thursday works."

"It's settled then. We'll go after work on Thursday." Without another word, he turned and left. Seconds later, I heard his Mercedes speeding away.

I sat silent and digested what had just taken place. My boss had asked me out to dinner. I know he'd given a different and valid reason for wanting to take me out, but I wasn't a fool. I'd seen a hidden agenda in his eyes. So why did I say yes? I was curious to know what they thought, yes, but had I a hidden agenda as well?

I looked at Stephen's picture. He was my man, my lover, my best friend, now turned stranger. I should have said no. Again, should have focused on making the stranger a friend again. But I hadn't.

My cell phone rang suddenly. I looked at the display and then answered. "Hey."

"Hey," Stephen said. "How much longer are you going to work?"

"I don't know. Why?"

"Because we haven't had dinner together for a while. I was hoping we could do that and talk."

"Talk about what, Stephen?"

"Us. I want to talk about us. We need to figure out what direction we're going in. Shit's not right between us. Hasn't been right in a long time. I don't know about you, but I'm hoping things can change."

I sighed. I wasn't in the mood to talk. "Stephen, I have a lot of work to do. Let me call you back."

"You never call me back."

"I have to go. I'm not sure when I'll be out of here, so don't wait for me to eat."

"This bullshit has to change, Danita. We have to make it change."

"I'll call you when I'm on my way home, okay." I ended the call, sat back, and took a few deep breaths. I hated that things were so bad. I hated even more that I just couldn't give of myself the way he wanted me to—the way he was willing to give himself. I wanted to call him back and apologize, but I knew he'd want to talk more, and I just couldn't deal with that. I looked at his picture

again and then closed my eyes. In the darkness behind my eyelids, I saw Jeff's smile. It was so inviting, even if I didn't want to give in. Damn. I reached
for my desk calendar and grabbed my pen.

Under Thursday, I wrote, "Business dinner."

6

Jeff took me to Ruth's Chris Steak House in downtown Baltimore. We left an hour after the office had closed. We drove separate cars, because it wasn't a date in my eyes, so there hadn't been a need to travel together. After I had called Stephen and told him that I was meeting Latrice and Emily for a spontaneous girls 'night out, I left. I felt guilty for doing so, but the argument Stephen and I had had over the phone when I had called, helped to make my decision a little easier.

"Danita, don't you want to work things out between us?"

"Stephen, not now. Please, can we have one night without us going down this road?"

"I don't like this road any more than you do, but I'm willing to take my shoes off and moonwalk if it'll help."

"I have to go. Please, let's do this later."

"Later when? You're going to come home, go to sleep, and then the routine that we've fallen into will start all over again in the morning. We wake up, leave for work, don't speak or see each other until the evening, come home, and go to sleep. So you tell me when later will be, because I sure as hell don't know."

"Just later, Stephen."

"Right. Later. Later when it's convenient for you, I guess, right."

"Damn, Stephen."

" 'Damn Stephen', what? What do you expect me to do? Or better yet, what should I do? Since you so obviously want to control how our relationship progresses, or doesn't progress, you tell me what I should fucking do."

"Whatever the hell you want."

"Right. If that was the case, you'd be coming home, and we'd be dealing with this shit. That's all I want to do. Damn baby, don't you want to change things? I don't understand how you can say to me day after day that you love me, but you're not willing to take some time and talk to me."

"Talk. That's all we ever do. I'm tired of talking."

"No, I talk. You just roll your eyes and check the time, letting me know that you'd rather be doing anything, but that. Can't you just skip this night out and come home? You've worked late every night this week. We've barely seen each other. I'm tired of only catching a glimpse of your back as you sleep."

"I'm tired too, Stephen."

"Then come home. Forget Latrice tonight. She'll live. Lady, we're losing all that we have. Don't you care?"

"Of course I care. Shit. Can we just do this some other time? I don't want or need this right now."

"Whatever, Danita."

He hung up then, leaving me massaging my temples. I reached inside of my purse and took two Advil from the bottle. I was one step away from changing my mind about the dinner, but after that conversation, I grabbed my keys and headed to my car. I called Jeff on his cell phone and told him that I was on my way.

I headed down 95 and cruised to Baltimore city doing eighty-five. It was December, and snow still hadn't fallen yet, but it was cold. I had the heat turned up and pointed at my feet.

When I got to Ruth's Chris, I let the valet park the car, and then walked inside. Jeff was already at the table waiting for me. He put up his hand and waved at me when he saw me. I walked to the table and removed my leather coat, threw it over the back of an empty chair beside me, and sat down. I was wearing my long black skirt with slits at the sides, and a red blouse. I was looking good. And this was just a business dinner, I'd told myself.

"Sorry I'm so late. I got tied up with something."

He gave me that damn smile again. He wasn't wearing the casual clothing that he normally wore. Instead, he had on gray slacks and a black button-down shirt. On the back of his chair was the matching gray blazer. I'll be honest—he looked smooth. Again, I reminded myself that this was just a business dinner—even if we were eating in one of the most expensive restaurants in all of Baltimore, where spending just over a hundred was considered a cheap dinner.

"You're not late at all. You're right on CP time. It's all good."

I chuckled at his joke and then grabbed a menu. "So have you ordered anything yet?"

"No. I was waiting for the main course to get here first."

Smooth. I had to give him that. He knew how to use the word play. I blushed and kept my eyes focused on the selections in the menu. I chose to ignore his comment, although I had heard it loud and clear. After deciding on the steak, I closed the menu and took a sip of water and then looked at him, which I immediately regretted. He stared at me with his soft gray eyes, which only appeared more spectacular in the lighting from the restaurant.

It wasn't easy, but I forced myself to look away. From the corner of my eye, I think I saw him give the faintest of smiles. I kept my eyes fixed on the ice cubes in my glass. "So, are you and Will pleased with my work so far?"

Out of nowhere, he leaned his head back and laughed out loud.

"What's so funny?" I was a little annoyed by his actions.

"You," he said simply.

I looked at him. "Me? I didn't hear myself crack any jokes."

He laughed again. "You are extremely funny, Danita."

I eyed him. "Well, why don't you tell me what kind of a comedian I am?"

He stopped laughing then and just stared at me, actually making me a little uneasy. "You know I didn't ask you out to discuss business."

"You didn't?" I watched him as he watched me. I'd taken his bait—perhaps willingly—and now he wasn't holding back. I said, "You're married, Jeff." I'd kept my voice low to keep anyone else from hearing our conversation.

"And you're here."

I shook my head. "Jeff, I'm involved."

He intertwined his fingers on the table. "And you're still here."

Damn. Why did the brother have to look so damn sexy? Why couldn't he have been just plain old Jeff? Of course, it was plain old Jeff who'd asked me out.

"We can't go there, Jeff."

He turned his palms to the ceiling. "We've already taken one step."

"It should be our last."

He intertwined his hands again. "There aren't any brakes."

Stop coming up with smooth responses, damn it!

I laid my palms flat on the table. "Jeff, this isn't right. You're my boss. You're married with kids. You follow me so far?"

He just smiled. "You get more attractive each time I see you, Danita."

Damn. Flattery will get you everywhere.

I shook my head. "Jeff . . . we can't—"

He laid his hand on mine. "In this lighting, you eyes are even more beautiful."

Do tell.

No, no, no!

I pulled my hand away slowly. "Jeff, we're coworkers. We need—"

"You know, I was taken by you the first time I saw you in that conference room."

"I know."

I looked away from him. My thoughts were slipping out.

"Oh, you did, did you? And what did you think of me?"

With a serious glare, I said, "I didn't like you."

"I know."

I tilted my head slightly. "Oh, you did?"

He laughed again and took a sip of his water. I watched him drink. I watched his Adam's apple move up and down as he swallowed.

"I thought you were arrogant," I said.

He touched my hand again. "And what do you think now?"

This time I didn't pull away. "That you're arrogant."

He laughed and shook his head. "I'm not arrogant. I'm confident. There's a big difference between the two."

I withdrew my hand and crossed my arms against my chest, curling my lips. "Is there?"

"Yes. Being arrogant makes one ignorant. Being arrogant means thinking that you are the shit to end all shit. I'm neither one of those things. I'm comfortable with myself as a man and comfortable with my abilities as a lawyer, husband, father, et cetera. Confidence, Danita. Big difference."

"I see. I'll have to remember that."

Our food came after that. Jeff ordered steak also—medium rare. I had mine well-done. We switched topics as we ate. Spoke about the recent death of the Washington Redskin Sean Taylor. "It was really sad and senseless," I said rubbing my arms. Talking about death always spooked me.

"For him to have been so young and to just really be making the transition to becoming a man is awful."

Jeff nodded. "I know what you mean. We lost several brothers that day. Sean and the three assailants whose lives will never be the same."

"When things like that happen, it makes you realize that despite money and fame, no one can avoid the Grim Reaper. None of us are immortal. We're all given a life span, and none of us know how long or short it's going to be."

He agreed. "No, we don't. That's why sometimes we have to grab at whatever opportunities come before us."

I lowered my head and went back to my steak. We were silent for a little while after that, and then we actually spoke about work. He told me about certain cases he had going, and for the first time, asked me how I liked the job. I told him I liked it very much, although the phones and Rodney, with his ugly ass, had been getting on my nerves. He laughed and said that it would all be changing soon, then left it at that. I didn't press.

For the rest of the evening, we spoke about anything but he and me. I made sure of it. Politics was cool, sports great—anything but what he wanted to talk about. It made me think of Stephen and how I did the same thing with him too. Maybe there'd been some validity to Stephen's comment about control.

When we both finished eating, Jeff paid the bill with the company credit card, and then looked at his watch. I did the same. It was past midnight! I looked around the restaurant and saw that we were the only people left.

"We should go and let these people go home. They're probably fuming at us right now."

As slick as oil, Jeff took my hand in his again. "It's okay. We can stay all night if we wanted to."

I looked at him, but didn't pull my hand away. His hand was so warm and soft. "Oh really?" I whispered.

"Really. The owner is a former client of mine. I helped him win half a million dollars for a hit and run with a trucking company. Time is not an issue."

I felt goose bumps run up and down my arms, neck, and back, and cleared my throat. I had to get a grip. I pulled my hand away, very slowly, and grabbed my coat and purse and stood up.

"Well, I'm sure that it's an issue for your wife and my man. I have to get going."

He stood up and grabbed his blazer. "Let me walk you to your car."

I put up my hand. I couldn't let that happen. Too much had already happened as it is. "It's all right. I did valet parking. They'll bring my car right to me. Good night, Jeff. Thank you for dinner." Without saying anything else, I left.

As I drove away, I breathed a sigh of relief. I welcomed the cold, because I had been hot. It had been close. I'd almost slipped.

When I got home, Stephen was up and sitting in the living room in the dark listening to a Howard Hewett CD. I walked in and listened to the words. Three lines in particular really affected me.

When the song finished, Stephen shut off the CD player and looked at me. I was ready for the twenty questions that he usually asked after I had come home from going out, but he didn't say a word.

I stared at him. Tried to read his mind. He didn't give away anything, which for a man who wore his emotions on his sleeve the way he did was pretty amazing.

Stephen put down the remote control to the stereo and rose from the sofa. His face was a stone as he walked past me and said, "Good night."

When I heard the bedroom door close, I went to the stereo and pressed play on the CD player. I skipped ahead to song number seven. As Howard sang to me, I sat on the sofa and cried.

7

Although I tried my best to prevent it from happening, Jeff and I eventually started seeing each other. We took advantage of all the moments we could. We started spending lunches together. Occasionally, we would mix it up and include other people from the office, just to make it look good. If we couldn't do lunch, we would see each other for a little while after people had gone home. On weekends, we would both go in when no one else was there. It took a couple of months before we became intimate. We didn't share our first kiss until New Year's Day. That was the turning point for us. Before that kiss, I was too scared to do anything. There were too many things to think about. So many people that could be hurt.

So I did what I thought was best—took it slow. Let the time pass and let our affair blossom. We cruised through October, slowed for some turkey in November, and exchanged gifts in December.

He bought me a diamond pendant and earrings that would have cost me my whole paycheck. I told Stephen that Latrice had bought them for me. Said that we gave each other jewelry this year. I bought Jeff some cologne.

We exchanged our gifts after everyone had left work early to go home on Christmas eve. We couldn't see each other because he had his obligations, and I had mine.

That was another issue.

My relationship with Stephen had become like a seesaw. One day it was okay and rising high, and the next, or sometimes the same day, it was back on the ground.

And it was all my fault.

Stephen tried everything he could do for us to be in love like we used to be. He was willing to go the extra distance required to make things work. But it was all in vain, because, even though I'd pretty much moved on past the condom issue, as much as I hated to admit it, I could feel myself falling more and more for Jeff.

Things did pick up for Stephen and me during the holiday season, though. The seesaw was up in the air during December. We had fun shopping for gifts for our friends and family, and each other. He bought me an expensive Coach bag, some new workout clothes for the gym, and a beautiful onyx necklace. I bought Stephen a bucketload of clothing, a pair of speakers for his car, and a digital camera for his computer. We had Christmas eve dinner with my mama, which was rough, because I felt like she was analyzing us the whole time we were there. I made sure to put on a good act, though. I was Miss Lovey-Dovey the whole time. I didn't want to give any impression that we were at odds. For Christmas dinner, we went to Stephen's parents' house and ate there.

We had fun. I adored his family. His mother was like a second mom to me. She wanted Stephen and me to have children someday. She was always asking when her grandkids were coming. I helped her finish the preparations in the kitchen, while Stephen, his father, and his brother, Kyle, watched football on the new big-screen television his parents had bought for themselves.

I wish the holidays could have lasted year-round. Stephen and I were so happy. But despite the high we were on, I still couldn't get Jeff out of my mind. And after our kiss, things had just taken off from there. We began speaking every moment we could. I loved to hear the sound of his voice. I'd call him in the morning on the way to work. He'd call me when he was out of the office, or we'd speak after work. When we could, we would go out. Of course, all Stephen knew was that I was out with Emily and Latrice.

Jeff was not the man I had expected him to be. He was romantic and sensitive. He made me feel like I was as special as he told me I was. I loved the little things he would do. Like leaving Post-it notes with messages that only he and I would understand. Or like leaving voice mails on my cell phone, letting me that know he was thinking about me. Day after day, he would take another piece of my heart and add it to his. Stephen tried also, but his piece would always break before he could claim it.

The distance between us was a mile long now, and

growing. And no matter what we tried, we couldn't seem to get things right. I wasn't happy with myself over what was happening. Some nights, as we lay in bed, Stephen would be watching TV or reading, and I would just look at him. He was a good man. My mama was right about that. And he did love me with all of his heart. I could feel that when he was with me.

Like any man, or person for that matter, he wasn't perfect. He had his ways about him—ways that just seemed to get to me the closer I got to Jeff. For one thing, Stephen could be very possessive at times. Sometimes, I felt like he didn't want me to go any-where without him. Felt like he didn't trust me. Until Jeff came along, he never had anything to worry about. I was his, and wanted to be, through sickness and health.

Something else about Stephen that worked me, which was most women's fantasy, was that he was always there for me—always ready to take care of me. It may seem strange and off the wall, but Jeff's cockiness and self-serving attitude kind of turned me on. I liked the fact that he took control some-times and dictated what we did, whether I wanted to or not. Like the dinner at Ruth's Chris. He wasn't taking no for an answer, despite the fact that I had made it plain as day that it wasn't a good idea. Well, at least I tried to. But I liked how he walked away and told me what day and what time, and moved on as if he had more important things to deal with. Stephen wasn't a pushover by any means. The Leo in him could be a stubborn bastard when he wanted to be. He just didn't have Jeff's machismo.

That's one of the main things I was feeling about Jeff. I loved to see him around the office, walking with his shoulders back and chest out, as if he were proclaiming himself the king. I was always excited when he was around. I liked to hear his sexy voice when he spoke on the phone from his office. When he wasn't around, I was always quieter, more reserved. I didn't think anyone had noticed. Until one day, Emily approached me. I was sitting at my desk typing a few form letters and listening to 96.3 WHUR.

"Hey girl," she said, tapping my shoulder.

I looked up at her. She was wearing a slamming black suit with a white lace top on. She had her hair styled in cornrows and was wearing a light shade of burgundy blush and eyeliner. Her lips were already a natural deep-wine color. It was the first time I had seen her all day.

"Whoa, where's Emily?" I said, looking past her. "Who are you? And what are you doing with Emily's body?"

She laughed and did a little pose. "You like the look?"

"Girl, I know you like the brothers, but there's no need for you to switch it up. They're already feening over your skin color. Don't you know it's in to be a white female?"

Emily and I laughed together. Hanging out with me and Latrice was definitely having an effect on her.

"What's up, girl? What do you need?"

Her eyes got serious, and her voice got quiet. She leaned toward me. "You have a minute to talk?"

I looked at her and saw no trace of a smile. I could tell we were going to need some privacy. I nodded and stood up. "It's not that cold today. Let's go outside. I need the break anyway."

She followed me, and as we walked past a few of the people, I swear they were staring at me harder than usual, as if they knew something I didn't know. "Will somebody fill me in?" I said, walking past them and through the door.

Emily and I stayed close to the building, but off to the side, so we were away from the smokers. Emily wrapped her arms tightly around herself.

"I thought white people liked the cold?" I said.

"Sheeeit," she answered.

Damn, she picked that up from Latrice too.

"So what's up, Em? You look like you have a lot on your mind. You having problems with your man?"

Emily shook her head. She did look good with her hair cornrowed. "No, Darius and I aren't having problems. And he is *not* my man, thank you very much. I belong to no man."

"Don't forget about the one upstairs."

"Well, he's a given."

"True. So what's weighing you down?"

"Danita, I'm going to ask you something, okay? I don't want you to get mad, but I need to know something."

I looked at her and slit my eyes. I didn't like the vibe she was sending off. "Okay."

Emily took a deep breath and then very quietly said, "Are you and Jeff sleeping together?"

I held my breath and felt my heart do a double step. Damn. Had we been obvious? Had anyone seen us together? Had we been overly friendly in the office? Or not friendly enough?

I looked at Emily. "What? Uh . . . uh. You didn't just ask me that, did you?"

"Look, I'm your friend, all right. I care about

you. It's just that rumors are going around that you and Jeff are getting it on."

"Rumors? Getting it on? Who the hell is saying this? What bitch is trying to ruin my reputation?"

"I don't know, Danita. I just heard that."

"Well, who did you hear it from?"

"I can't say."

"Can't say? What do you mean, you can't say? Someone is trying to ruin my good name, and you can't tell me? Your own friend who you just said you cared about? What's up with that?" I folded my arms across my chest and stared at her dead in the eye. On the outside, I was serious and angry, but on the inside I was screaming. Emily looked like she was about to cry with me all up in her face. I hated having to go off like that, but I had to keep up the facade.

"Danita . . ." Emily's voice was cracking. "I am your friend. You know that. But I don't want to be involved in anything. Because it was a rumor, I wanted to ask you for the truth, and I wanted to let you know what people were thinking."

I curled my lips and raised an eyebrow. She had my back, and I appreciated that. "Mmm, huh. I see. Well, to answer the rumor, no, Jeff and I aren't fucking. We work together, that's all. Just because we occasionally have lunch together, that doesn't mean anything."

"I know. I just had to ask."

"Well, you asked, and now you know."

When we went back inside, and for the rest of the afternoon, I could feel everyone's eyes and ears trying to catch a peek and a whisper of anything I was doing or saying. Got on my damn nerves so bad, I felt inclined to give out a few nasty stares. As I drove home, I called Jeff on his cell and told him what happened.

He laughed. "Let them think what they want."

I pressed down on the gas pedal in anger and cruised past an old woman who drove like she was racing a turtle. "I don't think anything is funny, Jeff," I said, blowing my horn.

"What? It is. It's amazing to see how people can't mind their own business, but want to mind everyone else's. Well, if they want to think something . . . fuck 'em. It makes it easier for us."

"How do you figure that?"

"Because, now we can go out and not have to sneak around. We make it known that we heard about the rumor, and then do what we normally do. The validity of the rumor will be questioned because we're not hiding anything."

"I don't know. What if someone says something to your wife? I don't want the drama."

"Don't worry about my wife. I have that wrapped up tight like a mummy."

"Oh, do you?"

"Come on now, you know me."

"I certainly do."

"All right, then."

"Who do you think started it all?"

"It was probably Jai."

"Jai. Why her?"

"Because she has a thing for me."

"I heard she's a lesbian."

"Nah, she's bi."

"How do you know?"

"What? You think she doesn't watch me from

the corner of her eye every chance she gets? You think she doesn't flirt with me? She's bi, and she likes me. And don't think Renea doesn't know that. That's why she's so crabby all the time."

"Hmmph. I see. I'll have to watch next time." I was trying to hide my jealousy. I couldn't help but wonder if he had taken her skinny ass to dinner.

That night, as Stephen lay asleep, I lay next to him and wondered about what kind of things were being said about Jeff and me. I tried to figure out if we had done something to give off the impression that there had been something going on. I wondered if we had ever been seen together, but I didn't think that was possible because we were always careful in that respect. Whenever we met somewhere, we always went to a place where there was no chance of anyone we knew seeing us together. If we met for lunch, we drove separate cars. That way, whenever we came back to work, the perception would be that he was coming from his way and I was coming from mine. And when we were in the office, we were strictly business. We never, at least in my mind, let on that we had any other type of relationship other than employee and boss. So who could have known?

Jai?

What if Jeff had been right about her? What if she had been the one who started the rumors because she'd been a jealous bitch? Maybe she hadn't seen anything at all and just wanted to ruin my shit because I had Jeff's attention and she didn't.

Damn.

Then I got worried. If she was willing to go to those lengths to get me, how much further would she go? I looked at Stephen as he stirred on his side. We used to hold each other when we slept. Now, we faced opposite directions.

Jai.

As I watched my man sleep, I wondered about who that bitch had in mind to tell next.

8

After my talk with Emily, the atmosphere at the office changed. I felt like I was under a magnifying glass, being studied and analyzed. Every thing I said or did seemed to be scrutinized to the letter. I felt like I couldn't even go to the bathroom without something being said or whispered. I heard mumbled statements like, "Humph, I wonder where she's going," or, "I wonder who she's going to meet."

I couldn't get away from the shit. I thought about Jeff's suggestion that Jai may have started the rumors. I looked at her conceited ass from time to time, and caught her staring dead at me with evil eyes, like she was daring me to say something. I wanted to, but I kept my tongue in check, because I didn't know for sure who knew what. And I couldn't take the chance. But if there was one person to keep at the top of my list, she was definitely the one. But then she wasn't the only one who didn't hide their displeasure. I got accusatory glares from all angles. Even Tanya, with her old ass, got in the mix. I caught her rolling her eyes and curling her lips while she huddled with Jai by the water fountain. I guess she had decided to come out of her shell. Henry too had changed, as he went from being a partner in crime that I could joke around with, to avoiding me, acting like he didn't have time to spare. Like his ass ever did a lot of work anyway.

Even Emily had changed. She tried to act like everything was cool. Pretended that my answer to her question had been good enough for her. She even had my back in the office, often times saying out loud, "What? Do y'all have a problem with your eyes? You want her to leave a log of what she does for you?"

I had to admit, she put up a good front. She had enough attitude to almost be believable. Almost. But I could tell that she had her doubts too. I could see it in her eyes when she looked at me. That hurt. As Latrice devoted more time to Bernard, Emily and I had gotten closer. We'd hung out, kicked it after work a few times, and chitchatted on the phone at night a couple of times. But like Henry, her time had become precious.

Rodney seemed to be smiling a lot more lately. I just didn't know if maybe his wife had decided to give his fugly ass a piece, or if he was just enjoying my drama. I figured on the latter. The only person who didn't seem to have a problem with me was Renea. She actually flashed smiles and stopped by a few times to have short, but pleasant, conversations with me. But any fool could see that she wasn't on the level with her act. I knew the only reason she had become cool with me all of a sudden was because she believed something was going on between me and Jeff. I'm sure she was only too happy to see that his attention was no longer on Jai. That is, if it had ever been on her to begin with. The only person who never gave a clue as to whether or not they thought anything was going on, was Will. He just went about his everyday routine. I didn't know what to make of that.

With the rumors and suspicions flying around, I couldn't help but be on edge. I couldn't relax by myself or with Jeff. Although it was a hard thing to do, I knew I had to tell Jeff that we needed to cool things for a while. I also knew that he wasn't going to like the idea, but it was something I had to do. I waited until after everyone had left the office, hoping that it would be easier for me to talk. But it wasn't. Even though there were no other cars in the parking lot, I was still nervous about who could be watching.

Jeff noticed my apprehension. He came up behind me and massaged my shoulders. "Danita, don't worry about them. Let them act how they want to act."

I pulled away from him. "But Jeff, you're not there. You don't have to deal with the stares or the comments, or the attitudes. I do. I can't stand dealing with these bitches and their shit."

"But Danita, they don't know anything."

"How do you know? How do you know that one of them didn't see something?"

"Because if one of them did, you'd hear a lot more than the whispering, and be getting a lot more than dirty looks. They're just jealous, that's all. Most of them have no life anyway. They need something to liven up their humdrum existences somehow. What better way to liven it up than to say that we're messing around?"

"But we are messing around, Jeff."

"We know that. They think that."

"And that's not a good thing."

"That's nothing to worry about."

"Nothing to worry about? Damn it, how can you be so nonchalant about this? You may have Marion wrapped around your finger, but I'm not that lucky with Stephen. If word ever got back to him . . . I don't even want to think about what could happen."

Jeff didn't reply to that comment. And I knew why. As built as he was, I'm sure he didn't think a run-in with Stephen would be a problem. But I knew better. Stephen was pretty on the outside, but all street on the inside. I'd seen his fighting skills before. On more than one occasion while we were out, he had been forced to defend his honor as a man. If there was one thing Stephen demanded, it was respect. And he was by far the most protective man I'd ever been with. Jeff may have had the size, but Stephen had no fear.

"Listen Jeff . . . I think that we should just calm down for a little while before anything gets out of hand. You know I don't want to, but I just think it's best right now."

"Danita, baby, let's not stop a good thing just because a few bitches can't mind their own fucking business."

"Again, Jeff, you don't have to deal with them like I do."

"Fuck it. I'll fire them if I have to."

"Stop tripping. You know you can't do that. You

need them, even if you don't want to admit it. They do a good job, except for Jai."

"Yeah, but she's nice to look at," Jeff said with a devilish smile.

I punched him hard in his arm.

"Damn, Danita. I was just kidding."

I looked at him with steel eyes. I wasn't buying that "just kidding" bullshit. "Jeff, let's just chill out for a couple of weeks. I want to be safe with this. Besides, it'll give us a chance to think."

"Think about what?"

"About whether or not we should continue with this."

He gave me a look that said "yeah right." He tried to get me to change my mind about taking a break, but as he saw that I wasn't going to, he eventually gave in.

"Whatever you want, Danita," he said, turning away from me. I could hear a light touch of anger in his voice.

"Don't be like that, Jeff. I just want us to do the right thing. The safe thing."

Keeping his back to me, he said, "What's safe and right, is you in my arms."

"But with everyone—"

"Everyone else can go to hell, Danita."

"Jeff, let's just take the time to think, all right."

"Whatever you want, Danita," he said, disgusted. He left then, without so much as a good-bye.

Our break lasted all of a week.

9

Stephen Maxwell

My girl was cheating on me.

I hadn't actually seen anything firsthand, but I knew it was happening.

The signs were there.

The lies were there.

I'd tried to deny it for the longest time, tried to blame my suspicions on my own insecurities. But I finally admitted it to myself. And damn if that shit didn't hurt. With every day that passed, I felt as though salt was being poured right into an open wound in my heart.

Because I was heartbroken—no doubt about that shit. It pissed me off too, because I swore I would never go through the whole heartache, heartbreak dance again. After my last relationship, I swore I wouldn't fall in love again, or at least if I did, I wouldn't make the same mistake by giving all of my heart.

Damn it, if I hadn't given it all to Danita.

Danita Evans—she was my girl. My heart. My love. My best friend. My one.

Oh, we all have that one.

You know, the one that we all dream about. The one we ask God to send to us so that we can be eternally happy and in love. Yeah, no doubt, Danita was my one.

I thought I had found the one with my ex, Angela. We were the envy of all couples. We were tight like that. No one and nothing could come between us—until I acted like less than a man and cheated on her. Slept with some girl, who didn't mean shit to me, and ended up getting chlamydia. Things were ugly. I had to admit to Angela what I had done because she had to get checked out too. She went off on me. Cursed me out, threw anything she could find at me. She was like a violent whirlwind gone out of control. After her initial rage had passed, she let me take her to the doctor; sure enough, she had it too. Things weren't the same after that. There was no trust coming from her whatsoever. She didn't even want me to touch her. For the longest time, I didn't. I quickly became good friends with my right hand.

Because we had been together for so long, and because I was begging for her forgiveness every chance I got, she decided to try and work things out with me. We survived that mess somehow, but our bond was weakened. Then Garfield Edmonds came along. He was the choir leader at the church Angela and I had attended. Actually, she attended— I just went because our relationship was falling apart. I figured, maybe if I went with her, things would get better. I was wrong.

I wasn't feeling the spirit like she was. I tried, but because God was never a real mainstay in my home when I was growing up, the message the pastor was delivering never really hit me like it was supposed to. But for Angela, it was different. She became all wrapped up like she was about to go to hell and the only way to save her soul was to throw herself into the word. She started reading the Bible every chance she got. When she was in high school, she and her girls had formed a singing group and signed on with a manager. They were on the verge of blowing up and being TLC before TLC ever became a name. But once church came along, it became evident that they would have to find someone to replace Angela.

On the real, it wasn't just the church that did it. That's where Garfield came in. He found out Angela could blow her ass off and started hounding her every chance he could about joining the church choir. Fed her bullshit lines about her voice being a gift from God and that she had been given that gift to spread His word. She eventually bought into Garfield's tired rap and quit the group. Like everyone else, I wasn't too happy about that, but my displeasure wasn't because she quit. It was for a whole other reason. See, I knew Garfield had ulterior motives. I knew he didn't just want her to join the choir. Nah, that short, pudgy brother wasn't that slick. I could see through the haze. I had played the same game before, and his was no different— just not as good. He definitely wanted Angela. He was feeling her like an itch that just wouldn't go away, and he did all he could to scratch it.

Unfortunately, the pain I had caused Angela

pushed her away from me and had her going straight in the direction of the church, which eventually led to Garfield. And the more I tried to make her understand what side of the playing field he was really on, the further away from me she went. She didn't want to hear anything I had to say. To her, Garfield was a nice cat with good values, and while I was trying to be the good guy, I quickly became bad in her eyes. That's why they ended up hooking up. The way I figured it, Garfield represented God, and I was naturally the Devil. I think losing her like that was God's way of punishing me for perpetrating when I went to those three-hour-long services.

As Angela and I split on bad terms, I was left alone to deal with one of the worst things I'd ever had to go through—heartbreak. I'd seen other people go through it, heard all of the horror stories—knew all the lyrics from songs. But I had no idea that it was going to be as bad as it was. I couldn't eat, couldn't sleep, and couldn't focus at work. I was twenty-five and having a breakdown. And I had no one to blame but myself. I never once thought that maybe Angela was selfish and materialistic. I never once thought that her unwillingness to compromise had anything to do with our breakup. As far as I was concerned, I deserved all of the pain and loneliness.

I was at rock-bottom emotionally for a good six months. I was going nowhere fast. Didn't try to excel jobwise, barely spoke to my boys, distanced myself from my family, and definitely wasn't trying to talk to any honeys. I just kept company with my misery. But as it usually does with time, my broken heart and old wounds started to heal slowly. I started to realize that life didn't begin or end with Angela Tremane. I got my focus back, started returning phone calls and answering e-mails. I even stepped back into the gym, a place I hadn't gone to during my entire bout of depression.

Six months later, I met Danita.

Months before that I had taken a project manager's position at E-Systems Communication. There I met Danita's best friend, Latrice Meadows. She hooked me up with Danita. Actually, she lied to me and told me that Danita wanted to meet me. I was in my cubicle working on a six-month projection plan for one of my accounts when she had approached me. I had been there for five months, and had been sweated by her since day one. I figured she was coming to ask me out for the umpteenth time. She surprised me when she said, "Go out with my girl."

I looked up from my screen and looked at her as she stared back at me, waiting for me to respond. "What's up, Latrice? How are you doing? You having a good day? I am, thank you."

"Ha-ha. Funny," she said.

"Yeah, I thought so. Now what's up with your demand you just made?"

"My girl, Danita, wants to go out with you. I'm telling you to go, because you two would be good together."

"Latrice, since day one, you been trying to get me to go out with you. If I keep saying no to you, which is nothing personal, what makes you think I'm going to say yes to going out with your friend, who I've never seen, never met, and never heard mention of before? And what do you mean, wants to go out with me? What have you told her?"

She rolled her eyes and flicked her wrist. "Her name is Danita Evans. She's a manager for the Limited in the Galleria. I've known her for over ten years. She's fine, got a body that you would appreciate with *your* picky ass. She's ten times smarter than Delia from provisioning—who you *never* should've messed with—her personality is all that, and she's light-skinned, which should make *you* very happy. There—now you've heard mention of her. You can see her tonight when you pick her up. And I said only positive things about you."

I had to laugh. Latrice was definitely one of a kind. Of all the people I worked with, she was the only one who had kept it real enough for me to want to get close. Although she liked me, and tried time and time again to get me to go out with her, she remained cool, even though I continuously turned her down.

"That's all right," she would say. "There's plenty of brothers who want these big thighs."

Big thighs. It wasn't just the big thighs she had. She had the hips, size-D breasts, an ass to sit on, and a few extra rolls. All in all, Latrice was a couple pounds short of a heart attack. Well, maybe not that bad, but she was pushing it. But she was cool as hell.

"What do you mean, when I pick her up? What did you smoke for lunch?"

"Ha-ha. You just keep coming up with the jokes today."

"Yeah. I'm a regular Chris Rock."

"Umm, no. Now, what time are you picking her up? Seven-thirty seems like a good time."

"Whoa, hold up. You need a Q-tip? Have you been listening to anything I was saying? I don't know your friend."

"You will after tonight."

"Latrice, I don't do blind dates."

"First time for everything."

"I don't do firsts."

"So, then take her out a second time and you can do her then."

"Oh, so you've got the jokes now?"

"I got a little sumthin', sumthin'."

"What's up with trying to hook me up? Do I have *desperate* taped to my back?"

"Come on, Stephen. You're a nice guy, somewhat attractive—"

"—What happened to being as fine as Denzel, except with a goatee and curly hair?"

She curled her lips and showed me the inside of her hand. "Like I said, somewhat attractive. And it's not that I'm trying to hook you up."

"Oh, it's not? Then what would you call what you're doing?"

"Stephen, look, ever since you came to E-Systems, you have either been alone or disgracing yourself with the worst of the litter you've been choosing from."

"Come on, now. They haven't all been that bad."

Latrice gave me a look that said, "yeah right." "You went out with Wanda from HR. Wanda! Her coochie's been driven through so many times they need to assign a street name to it. She's had more customers than McDonald's on a Friday night."

"I got you. But I didn't sleep with her."

"You still went out with her. Then there was Dawn from engineering."

I put up my finger. "Dawn's an attractive woman—"

"—With six kids, six different alimony checks from six different baby daddies, and she's looking for a seventh."

I opened my mouth to speak, but changed my mind. I couldn't disagree with her on that point, and I had slept with Dawn.

"And please, let's not discuss Delia. That was your low point. You were wearing the *desperate* tag then. Girl's so stupid, when she closes her eyes to go to sleep at night, she probably thinks she's going blind. How she ended up here is amazing to me. All she has is a body and braids. I think she needs to loosen up some of those fake-ass braids so her head can get some relief."

I couldn't hold back my laugh that time. I didn't even try. She was right about Delia. I was desperate and horny and went out with her, knowing how mentally challenged she was. I had been on a dry spell though, and was looking for a release, and got it—three times in one night. We never hooked up again, and anytime we saw each other, we only made small talk—never mentioned our romp. I think she was embarrassed because she had given it up so easily, and I just had no interest in her whatsoever.

"Just go out with Danita, Stephen," Latrice said. "You won't be disappointed. I'm not going to fix you up with some ugly trick. Besides, she's looking forward to meeting you."

I looked at Latrice and chewed on my bottom lip. It had been awhile since I had gone out on a date. Maybe it wouldn't be so bad.

"All right. I'll go out with her."

"Seven-thirty, right?"

"Yeah, seven-thirty is cool."

When I arrived at Danita's apartment, my hands were shaking with nervous anticipation. I couldn't believe I was actually about to take someone I'd never met out to dinner. "You've hit a new low, my brother," I whispered, walking up to her door. Before I had rung the bell, I took a deep breath. I was looking sharp in all black: black slacks, black form-fitting shirt, and black Kenneth Cole shoes. Then I had a thought—what if she answered the door looking like Cruella De Vil on a bad hair day? Nah, chill . . . she couldn't be that bad. Could she? Besides, most big girls had an attractive girlfriend. I was banking on that myth when I rang the bell and waited.

My heart tripled in beats when I heard the doorknob jiggle. When Danita opened the door, I felt my bottom lip fall to the ground—she was that fine. She was wearing a short black skirt, which showed off a pair of sexy, athletic legs. To complement the skirt, she wore a white sleeveless top. Her arms were defined, yet soft. She worked out, but didn't overdo it. I cleared my throat and averted my eyes from her body to her eyes. I almost got lost in their light brown sparkle. I cleared my throat again and said, "Hello, Danita."

She extended her petite hand. "Hello, Stephen."

I took her to the Rusty Scupper because my boy, Carlos, said it was a romantic spot, with a nice view of the harbor by candlelight. I'd never been there, so I figured this was as good a time as any to see if he was right. We sat by a window, with a clear view of the water, and talked for hours. After that, we walked the Harbor and talked some more. I felt comfortable around her, like I'd known her a lot longer than a few hours. Later that night, we exchanged numbers and were supposed to go out the next weekend. But I couldn't wait that long. I called her the next day and invited her out to the movies.

After the movies we ended up back at my place and watched the NFL Network. It was nice being around someone who loved football as much as I did. I even let the fact that she liked the New York Giants slide, which wasn't easy for me to do, being a die-hard Baltimore Raven fan. After watching *NFL Replay*, Danita got up to go. That's when things happened.

One minute, we were hugging, the next, we were caressing with our tongues. Then we were in my bed making love. And notice I said *making love*. Because that's exactly what it was. We took the kissing from the living room to the bedroom without missing a beat. There, she sat me on the bed and performed an erotic rhythmic dance as she removed her clothes piece by piece. My manhood was knocking at the inner walls of my pants, demanding to be let out. To avoid an argument, I let it out right away.

As I sat on the bed, naked and erect, I stared at Danita in all her splendor. Never had I seen a woman as naturally beautiful as she was. She had a dancer's build, with breasts, hips, and legs that curved in all the right ways. I couldn't remember ever being as excited as I was that night. I throbbed to her rhythm.

She slowly approached me, with a smile as seductive as her step, and straddled me. But she wouldn't let me enter her wet cavern. Instead, she began kissing me on my face, starting at my forehead. From there she moved to my neck and then to my chest. I pulsated with every kiss she was giving me. My hips moved to a slow grind. She suddenly stopped and stared at me. "I want you to know, I don't do something like this on the regular."

"I believe you," I said. I would've believed anything at that moment. She began stroking me and kept her eyes locked on mine.

"It takes a special man to get me like this," she said, making me harder than I'd ever been. "Are you that special man, Stephen?"

"I'd like to think so," I whispered in between a gasp.

"I'm not easy, you know," she said, staring and stroking.

"I never implied or felt that you were."

"I feel something with you. I can't explain it, but I do. I hope I'm not wrong."

"No, you aren't wrong at all." I exhaled and felt chills run up my spine. I inhaled her strawberry scent and kissed her neck. She continued to work her magic with her hands so well that I had to put my hand on hers and make her stop. "I don't want it to be over yet," I said.

"Don't worry about it. We have all night," she whispered.

After that, it was on. We took turns tasting each other's secret wine, making each other squirm, beg, and eventually climax. When our bodies were ready to go again, I slipped on a condom, and then we made slow, sweet, passionate love. I matched her grind with my stroke. I wanted her to feel as much of me as she could. Wanted her to see how much I wanted her. I could tell from the way she rode me that she wanted the same thing. When we were completely spent, we spooned under the sheets and went to sleep. Actually, she slept. I lay there and wondered where she had been all my life. Not since Angela had I felt that type of connection. Everything seemed so natural and meant to be.

We never cooled down after that night. We saw each other whenever we could; never hesitating to duplicate or surpass the level of passion we had reached. I was happier than I could ever remember. Just being around her was changing me. I held my head higher, walked with my chest out farther. When we went out, although it bothered me to no end, I was happy to know that brothers were checking her out. And, of course, the sisters couldn't help but feel jealous about her style. We did everything together. Cooked, watched movies, worked out. As each day passed, I was feeling more and more like I never wanted to let her walk out of my life.

I took her with me for the weekly Sunday dinner at my folks' house in Tysons Corner, Virginia. Danita was the first woman since Angela that I'd taken over there, and because my mother had liked Angela so much, and had always been angry about how I caused the relationship to fall apart, I was a little nervous. My moms can be judgmental and unfriendly at times, and she can sure as hell hold a grudge, so I wasn't sure how she was going to receive Danita when she opened the door. Knowing my Moms, I was ready for her slit eyes, a straight lip, and folded arms.

"Moms, this is Danita Evans."

"Danita. . . . Danita. I like that. Sweet name."

"Thank you, Mrs. Maxwell."

"Please, call me Rosalyn."

Her reaction surprised me. What shocked me even more was when she hugged Danita as though she'd always been part of the family.

"Mmm, hmm. You found yourself a winner, Stephen. You better not lose her." She stared at me hard when she said that. I nodded my head. I didn't plan on losing her anywhere.

She hugged Danita again, and I couldn't help but smile. As we stood in the doorway, my pops approached. He's a big man with squared shoulders and big hands. He was intimidating without even trying. Add that to the fact that he provided for his family like no man could, and he could swing a mean belt, it wasn't hard to see why I respected him so much—he was my idol. I hugged him and patted his back. "Hey, old man."

He smiled back at me. "What's up, son?"

We stared at each other for a few seconds. I get my height from him. I also have his lady-killing smile. I'd seen him turn heads with that smile. He finally looked past me and at Danita. "And who is this attractive woman you have here? She can't be with you? She wouldn't settle like that, would she?"

I laughed and grabbed Danita's hand. "This is Danita Evans. Danita, this old man who doesn't realize how fine his son is, is my pops."

Danita smiled and hugged my father like she had done it before. "Hello, Mr. Maxwell. It's nice to finally meet you."

"Nice to meet you too, Danita." He let her go

and smiled. "And please, Mr. Maxwell was my father. I'm just plain ol' Pops. And my son was wrong about something."

"What's that?" she asked.

"I do realize how fine my son is, because he got his looks from me."

We all laughed, and then my mother interjected, "And where was I when you gave him those looks?"

"Oh baby, you know I was just playing."

"Um, hmm. Well, why don't you take your playing behind over there and set the table with Stephen, while Danita and I go in the kitchen. I need to prepare her for life with my son."

I raised my eyebrows playfully. "Don't listen to a word she says, Danita. It's all lies. Lies, I tell you!" We all laughed and then my mother took Danita to the kitchen. As my pops and I prepared the table, I asked, "Where's Kyle?"

Kyle's my little brother by seven years. He was just starting his freshman year at University of Maryland. Even though he lived on campus, he always made it for Sunday dinner. I was surprised that he wasn't here already.

"Oh, Kyle's got some major studying to do. He has a big exam tomorrow. He had to duck out on us this time."

"Too bad. I was hoping to beat him in some *Madden* on the Xbox. You have been brushing up on your skills, haven't you?"

My father looked at me with a smirk. "You're leavin' here tonight with a good old-fashioned ass-kickin'. It's just a damn shame Danita has to see that."

"We'll see, old man," I said, giving him a light tap on his shoulder. "Speaking of which . . . I expected Moms to throw an attitude when she met Danita. I know she's still mad about what went down with Angela and me." I passed him a plate to set.

"Yeah, your mother was very disappointed with you. Angela was a good woman. She was good to you. Your mother loved her."

"I know she did. I know you cared for her too. I messed up. Plain and simple."

"Yeah, you did. And yeah, I did. The reason your mother didn't give you attitude is because one, I told her not to make Danita feel uncomfortable. And two, because she realized that if you were willing to bring her over for dinner, then you were serious about her. You've only ever brought one woman here."

I watched my father with serious eyes and then said softly, "I really do care about her, pops. She's special. I think she's the one."

My father patted my shoulder. "Well, all right. My boy is growing up."

We ate the scrumptious dinner that my mother prepared and then later that night my pops and I went head-to-head on the Xbox. He had definitely been working on his skills since the last time we had played. He beat me two out of three games. When Danita and I had left that night, he gave me some sound advice.

"Son, you need to work on your fingering skills. Study the book, work on your tackling and catching, then come back and see me." I smiled and left, promising myself that I would walk away the victor next time.

After the visit to my parents, Danita figured it was time for me to meet her mother. We went to her house for dinner. I had already spoken to her mother several times over the phone and already knew what she looked like from pictures in Danita's photo album. When we finally met, we hugged and spoke as if we'd always known each other. Her mother and I were alike in certain ways. We were both Leos, and like me, she strived for perfection. It showed in the food. She cooked baked chicken, mashed potatoes, green beans, and cornbread. By the time I was done eating, I felt like I added ten more pounds. Food was so good, I felt like I should've paid for it. When we left that night, I had a second mother.

Everything flowed for Danita and me. When I told my father that I thought she was the one, I had meant it. We eventually moved in together, after she had suggested it. Actually, she beat me to the punch, because I was going to suggest the very same thing. I know she was surprised when I agreed to the move, because I had told her early on that I wasn't going to commit myself to a woman like I had before. And I was serious at the time. But I had never felt more certain about anything or anyone like I did with her. As more and more time went on, I knew I wanted something deeper. I was ready to settle down. Me wanting to commit like that would have been a surprise to everyone but myself. I knew the time had come.

I told my longtime friend, Carlos, about my plans one night while we were out. Carlos and I had met at Hampton University and became instant friends. We started hanging out all the time.

Our personalities gelled. We loved the same type of music. Salsa, merengue, R&B, jazz, and hip-hop—and we both loved women. Early on, our goals for going out at night was to make sure that we didn't come back to the dorm without a fly honey on our arm.

"Yo kid, I'm gonna do it."

"Do what?" he said, eyeing a fine Latina sitting with a couple of her girlfriends. We were at the Silver Shadows nightclub in Columbia, chilling. It was Latin night there, and Carlos wanted to find himself a *chica*. I went because we hadn't hung out in a couple of weeks. We had both been busy with work. Carlos is an art teacher and a part-time counselor for troubled youths in DC. Hanging out was something we had both needed to do.

"I'm gonna buy a ring, kid."

Carlos looked at me with bug eyes. "What? Did you say *ring*? Maaaaaan, are you for real?"

I smiled. I was that happy. "Yeah kid, a ring. Things with me and Danita are too good, man. I can't let her go. It's time, bro."

"Shit. Time for you to get your head examined maybe. Nah for real, that's cool, man. I'm glad you found the right one for you. That's real cool."

"Thanks, man. I'm going tomorrow to start looking."

"You do that, bro." He looked back to the table with the girlies. He waved at the Latina, who waved back at him and smiled. If there was any one thing about Carlos that I could say, it would be that he loved women. And women loved his pretty-Ricky features and dark brown eyes. "Yeah, you do that, for real, bro," he said, turning back toward me.

"With you gone, that leaves more hens for me to peck."

"Kid, you need to settle down and find your one."

He looked at me like I had smacked him. "Settle down? Settle down? Bro, is you crazy? Why should I settle for my one, when I could have two, three, and four honeys? Settle down? Will somebody get this boy another drink?" We laughed and downed a couple of more beers.

When we had left the club, he was exchanging numbers with the girl he had been checking out. They had danced a couple of times throughout the night. Me, I stayed to myself and chilled. I wasn't trying to get caught up. I'd been down that road before and had no intention of going back. Besides, I couldn't get Danita off my mind. Carlos and I had left in my new Durango, which I had just recently bought, and went home.

The next morning, shit got ugly.

Danita shook me angrily and then yelled, "Stephen . . . Why do you have a condom in your pocket? What ho are you fuckin'?"

When I pulled the covers from over my head, she threw a condom at me. The night before, Carlos had been in my car going through his pockets for his house keys. Before he left, the condom slipped out and fell onto my seat. I found it as I was getting out of the car. I did the only thing I could do—told Danita the truth.

"The condom belongs to Carlos. He left it in my car." I figured that would've been enough for her. Hell, it should have been. But she surprised me when she went on.

"How convenient for you."

"It fell out of his pocket."

"And landed in yours, huh? What, were you unlucky in your quest for ass last night? Is that why you still have it? Or was this an extra one that you didn't get to use?"

Now, I was already tired from having been out, and I had a slight hangover, so the last thing I wanted was to argue. But I figured things would calm down after I gave her my answer.

That never happened.

I even offered to call Carlos to clear everything up. She didn't even want to do that. Talking about him having my back. Having my back for what?

My head was pounding from frustration and too much alcohol. I could only lay back and exhale to calm down. By this point, all hopes of sleeping my hangover off had gone away. I was pissed. As much as I loved her and spent time with her, she had the nerve to ask if I was fucking around on her.

I was ready to explode. There I was just the night before talking about how she had been the one and how I wanted to buy her a ring, and she could only accuse me of fucking somebody else. We argued back and forth, not really getting anywhere.

"You're kidding me, right? You're not really overblowing this, right?"

"Overblowing? Nigga, a condom fell out of your pocket and you give me the it's-a-friend's line?"

"Jesus Christ, Danita!" I yelled. "This is unbelievable!" I moved past her and went to the closet. I had to get the hell out of there.

"Where the fuck are you going? We're not finished."

"Danita . . . I'm finished. You can stay and argue all you want." To avoid saying the wrong thing, I kept my mouth shut and just got dressed quickly, and then grabbed my keys and left.

Things were never the same after that. And I never bought the ring.

10

The fact that Danita doubted my word about the condom pissed me off to no end. Although I could understand her apprehension and anger, I just couldn't believe she'd come at me that way. The next day, I met Carlos for a beer. For the sake of my own sanity, I had to get out of the house.

"Man, she didn't believe you?"

"She practically accused me, man. It was crazy. One minute I was sleeping, and the next she's asking me who I was fucking."

"Damn, bro. You want me to say somethin' to her? I mean, I don't know if it'll help, but I can."

I shook my head and sipped on my Corona. "Nah, man. Like you said, it wouldn't help. Besides, I offered to call you, and she wasn't having it."

"Damn. That's some ill shit. Of all the people in this world, the last person she should be suspicious of is you."

"I know that, and you know that. I thought she did too."

"So, what are you going to do?"

"Nothing," I said bluntly. "I told her the truth. What more is there for me to say?"

"I hear you, bro, but just remember . . . women can get evil—especially when they think their man is cheating."

"I hear you. But for real, that's Danita's own hang-up. Not mine."

After our conversation, I did exactly what I said I would do—nothing. I hadn't done anything wrong, and the last thing I was going to do was stress over it. I just wish that Danita had shared the same sentiment. Little by little, she had become more bitter and more distrusting. Although she never directly came out and said that she didn't trust me, I could read it in her eyes whenever she looked at me. I understood at first, because I had really made an effort to put myself in her shoes and look at the situation from her perspective. I was willing to do that. And yeah, I would've been mad as shit. I definitely would've wanted to break something if I had found a condom in her purse. I never faulted her for feeling the way she did. But what I did fault her for was not believing in me enough to see that I wasn't lying to her. That aggravated me. We had argument after argument, both trying to get the other to look at things from each other's side.

"Danita, why the hell do you keep sweating me about that damn condom? That was more than two months ago."

"Keep sweating you? Is that what you call it? Have you even tried to put yourself in my shoes? Have you once tried to see where I'm coming from? A condom, Stephen. A condom in your pants pocket after you went out the night before. A condom that you said was Carlos's. Do you have any idea how weak that sounds?"

"What do you want from me? I told you the truth. What more do you need? I even offered to call Carlos, but you refused."

"Uh, uh. I'm no fool. Ask Carlos, my ass. Like you and he wouldn't have already gotten together and gotten your stories straight. That condom was Carlos's all right. His ho ass probably gave that shit to you."

"Damn, Danita. If you don't want to believe me, then why stay with me? Shit, I told you the truth. What more do you want?"

Of course the argument when nowhere and once again, I grabbed my keys and left. I went driving just to drive and clear my head. Eventually, I ended up at Carlos's place. Although I had been driving around for an hour, I still wasn't ready to go home. When he opened the door, I stormed in.

"I'm tired of this shit, man!"

Carlos closed the door and turned to me. He was wearing a pair of sweats and had his hands taped. He'd been hitting his punching bag. "Come and hit the bag and tell me about it, bro," he said, heading back to his basement.

"Danita won't let up on this shit, man. It's driving me nuts!"

"Damn, bro. She's psycho with that shit," he said, holding the bag steady for me.

"Tell me about it."

"Women, bro. That's how they are. They always take things to the extreme."

I gave the bag a barrage of heavy blows that

threw Carlos off balance. "It just kills me that she won't take me for my word, man. I mean, as long as we've been together, you would think trust wouldn't be an issue."

"You would."

"Man, I've put so many miles on my car these past two months it's crazy." I hit the bag heavily, and again rocked Carlos backward a step.

"Sad thing, bro, is that if the tables were turned and you went psycho like her, you'd be here with bags in your hand."

"Yeah, no doubt about that," I said, giving the bag a couple of uppercuts.

"For real, man. Women can dish it out, but the minute a man tries to do the dishing—please. We become Public Enemy Number One. Females always have double standards when it comes to shit like that."

"Yeah, I know what you mean."

"Double standards, bro. Look at the women who call men dogs. They act like we're just supposed to accept their insults with a grain of salt. But what happens the minute we call them hoes? They get all ballistic and angry and shit, like it's not possible. Double standards, bro."

I pounded on the bag a few more times, until my hands started to hurt and then sat down on his workout bench. Carlos went upstairs and then came back down with two beers. He gave me one. "So, what are you goin' to do?"

I swallowed half the beer in one gulp. "I don't know, man."

Carlos tapped his bottle against mine. "The bag is here anytime you need it, bro."

"I appreciate that."

When I left his place and went back home, I sat in the living room and thought about Danita and her mistrust of me. It was just eating me up that she had taken things as far as she had. I fell asleep on the couch, and stayed there even after I woke up during the middle of the night. I was too pissed to even be near her.

Nothing was the same for us. Our communication completely died. We stopped being an open couple. Danita started going out without me more, and wouldn't tell me where she was going or when she was coming back. To put even more salt in the wound, our love life began to change. This was definitely not my doing. Danita went from being the queen of passion and romance to being indifferent and cold. She showed zero emotion in the bed, and I couldn't make her orgasm like I used to, because she wouldn't let herself go. It was fucking with me. Naturally, I became suspicious. I couldn't help but wonder if she was out and about, doing the do with some other brother, trying to get even for something I didn't do. And then when she started keeping things from me—maaaaan . . .

"Carlito, man, I'm stressed over this shit. I'm beginning to wonder if she's fucking around on me."

"Damn, bro! You think she would do that?"

"Don't know, man. She's sure as hell not being up-front about shit."

Carlos laughed. "Maybe *you* should be the one to go off on *her* now."

"Yeah, maybe I should.

"Yo, I like Danita, bro. She's cool. But maybe, and I know you may not want to hear this, maybe you need to move out and get some space in between you two. Give her time to come to her senses, bro. Give yourself time to figure out if being with her is really worth it."

"I don't know, man. As far as I go, I think it's worth it. We're good together. But her coming to her senses ain't gonna happen. As far as she's concerned, I fucked around on her. She's in tunnel-vision mode, man. She can't see or hear anything else."

"And she still won't ask me about it?"

"Kid, come on. Look how long we've known each other. Would you lie for me if I asked you to?"

"Come on, bro. You know I got your back."

"Exactly. She knows that too. So if my word doesn't count, you know yours ain't gonna mean shit."

"Damn. You're in a fucked-up situation. I wish there was something I could do. It's like this shit is all my fault or something."

"Nah, you didn't do shit."

"And neither did you. Yo, does she know you were going to buy a ring? You didn't buy the ring, right?"

"No, to your first question. Hell no, to your second. Telling her where I wanted to take our relationship wouldn't do a thing. And with us on the verge of breaking up, the last thing I'm gonna do is waste my money on a ring."

"Just checking, bro."

"Don't worry, man. I didn't lose my common sense yet."

"So, what are you going to do?"

"Carlito, I have no idea. So much has changed between us. We don't speak, we yell. We don't do together, we do apart. Man, we don't even have sex the same anymore."

"Word? You don't have sex?"

"Oh, we have sex. Only problem is it's like being with a stranger when we do. She's so damn unresponsive."

"Bro, you know once the sex starts to go—"

"—Yeah, I know. Everything goes with it."

"Damn straight. Sex and relationship go hand in hand. It's like a marriage between those two. When one goes, you can forget the rest. I couldn't be in a relationship with bad sex, bro. As much as I like to get my groove on. Shit, like I said to you before, you're a better man than I am. For real. As bad as you say it is . . . Kid, I would've been tappin' somethin' on the side already. Fuck that bad-sex, no-sex bullshit. My ass would've been on the next train to ho'ville the minute I wasn't being satisfied the right way. Plus, she don't want to trust your ass . . . That's why I will never settle down, bro. I can't handle the stress. You can have all that up-and-down mess."

"I don't mind the mess so much, man, as long as it can be fixed."

"Well, let me ask you, bro . . . Can it be?"

I didn't answer him, because I didn't know.

11

Somehow Danita and I had managed to stay together, but it wasn't easy. One minute we were in love, and the next, we were at each other's throats. I couldn't stand the stress. I wanted to work things out between us. I still wanted to buy that ring, because I still believed in us. I knew it was going to require work, though, but I was willing to do that.

As we struggled in our relationship, we also had to deal with our daily functions. Like work. My job was becoming increasingly more frustrating. As the economy slowed, so did E-System's growth, and instead of hiring, they started firing. People got laid off in waves, a couple of months at a time. It was an uneasy feeling to go to work and watch the people you worked closely with leave for a meeting and never come back to their desks. It was even more troubling to have to sit there and wonder when your turn was coming. Raises and bonuses had been put on a freeze, and needless to say, the morale within the company was low. We were all walking on eggshells, doing double the work with no incentive. What used to be a fun and exciting environment had become uncomfortable and unfriendly. Everyone seemed to have adopted the CYA attitude—cover your ass. Not that I really did before, but I really couldn't trust anyone now.

That especially applied to Latrice.

Now, even though she never let on, I was sure that she knew about the problems Danita and I were having. Danita had never hesitated to share anything with her before. She probably knew all about our sex life, as nosy as Latrice could be. But that didn't really bother me, because I understood the value of having friends to talk to, and I did the same with Carlos. But it did make me uncomfortable when she was around; she was a woman, and I fully expected her to take Danita's side. So at work, I had been avoiding going by her side of the building whenever I could. I didn't want to see the accusation I'd see in her eyes.

So, I was certainly surprised when she had come up to my cube one morning and invited me out to lunch. At first, I was going to say no, because I didn't want to deal with anything. But then I decided—fuck it. I'd listen to what she had to say and then just tell her to mind her own business.

We decided to head to Macaroni Grill. In the car, neither one of us said a word. I didn't know what she was thinking about, but my mind was just going over different versions of the discussion about Danita I was sure we were going to have. At the restaurant I watched her eyes, looking for an indicator as to when she was going to bring Danita's name up. The waiting was irritating me. I just wanted to get things over with. It didn't ease my mind any when she brought up the job.

"So," she said, sipping on her Diet Pepsi. "We've survived the cuts so far."

I nodded. "Yeah, so far. I'm worried about the next time, though."

"Well, I hear they won't be layin' anybody else off for at least another couple of months."

"Yeah, I heard that. But you never know."

"It's a damn shame that this had to happen to people now. Christmas is just a couple of months away."

"Yeah, it was pretty pathetic to do people like that. From what I understand, the severance packages haven't even been that good."

"I heard Delia was let go."

"Oh really," I said, not really caring.

"Yeah, I heard she made a big fuss about it and started making threats."

"She's full of talk."

"Yeah, but they're still nervous about it. I hear they've been watching her, making sure she don't come back. They boxed all her things up and mailed it to her."

"Damn, for real?"

Latrice shrugged her shoulders. "Hey, people are crazy nowadays. The last thing they or any of us want is for some psycho to walk in and go postal."

"True."

"You have a lot of stock?"

"A couple thousand shares. But I don't really watch it too closely because the stock market is shit right now. What's ours worth—a little under two dollars now?" I said, shaking my head.

"Yeah, I feel you on that," Latrice said, nodding.

We both got quiet then and put all of our attention back on our food. It was an uneasy kind of silence. I could see it in her eyes that she had something to say. Finally, I put my fork down. "Latrice, why'd you ask me out to lunch?"

Latrice swallowed the last of her pork wrapped in bacon and sighed. "Look Stephen, I know about what's going on with you and Danita."

I stared at her. "I'm sure you do."

Latrice kept her eyes locked with mine. "Danita's my girl, I've known her for a long time—"

I put my hand up. I didn't want to hear anymore. "Latrice, look, you're cool, so don't take this the wrong way, all right, but what's going on is between Danita and me. Believe me, I'm getting enough shit from her. The last thing I want is to be chastised by you." I sighed and cracked my knuckles. I could tell by her glare that she didn't like the tone of my voice, but I couldn't help it. Just thinking about the shit with Danita was pissing me off. I was in no mood to have to defend myself for doing nothing wrong.

She put up her index finger. "Hold up. First of all, I'm not trying to be all in your business. But Danita is my friend, and if she comes to me with her problems, then I'm going to listen. Second of all, I'm not even trying to chastise you. Truth be known, I believe what you told her was the truth."

I raised my eyebrows. "You do?"

"Yes, I do. I know you love her. I know how much time you devote to her. You're a good guy, and I honestly don't think you would do that to her. I hope I'm not wrong."

"You're not," I said looking at her seriously.

She kept eye contact with me. "Good. So, have you told her how you feel about everything?"

"Yes, I have. But as you already know, Danita can be a stubborn bitch sometimes. Especially once she's made up her mind about something, which she has already done about me."

"Look, you know she's been hurt bad in the past. Not just once, but a couple of times. I've tried to warn her about it, but she has a knack for holding onto the past, especially when it comes to things that happen in relationships."

I nodded. I knew that Danita had gone through difficult times with her previous lovers, although I had never known to what extent because she would only give out so much information.

I jabbed my index finger on the tabletop. "But I'm not any of those men. And this relationship isn't like her other ones."

"She knows that. But let me tell you, once a woman's been burned, it's awfully hard to forget. Especially when they're in love."

"Latrice, we're slowly falling apart. Does she want that to happen?"

"No, she doesn't. But she's scared. She needs time."

I sighed. "Enough time has passed. We should've been past this by now."

Latrice shrugged her shoulders and took a sip of her soda again. "Did you know she was having problems at work?"

"Yeah. She told me about how they fired the district manager and how she's had to pick up the slack with everything."

"Yeah, and they don't want to compensate a sister. Want her to bust her ass, but don't want to pay her."

"It's like that everywhere," I said. "I've spoken to her about trying to look for something else. But she doesn't think she's qualified enough."

"Yeah, well, I had a talk with her about that. Actually, I have a friend who works at a law firm. I passed Danita's résumé on to her and put in a good word."

"Really? This is news to me. She never mentioned it."

"Probably didn't want to get her hopes up. Anyway, my friend, Emily, called me today and told me that they had called Danita for an interview tomorrow."

"A law firm, huh? What's the position for?"

"She'll be answering the phones for them. She'll make better money than at that damn mall."

"That's good. Thanks for lookin' out for her."

Latrice laid her palms on the table. "Just give her some time. I think she'll come around."

I took Latrice's advice and gave Danita just that. Unfortunately, the new job just seemed to give her more of an excuse to put distance between us, and before Thanksgiving came and went, and before Christmas breezed by without so much as a pause, I began to notice another change in her. One that had been different from before.

When I had mentioned to Carlos that I felt Danita had been messing around on me, I'd only been half serious. I was willing to blame those feelings partly on my own insecurities and what we were going through. But as we stepped into the new year, something told me that my suspicions had been too real.

12

The first time I really became suspicious of Danita was on New Year's Day. We were supposed to go to my parents' house for dinner that evening, because the night before we had been with her mother and a few other relatives. We had always split up the holidays like that to be fair. During the day, I was running around on some errands for my parents, while Danita was making a peach cobbler to take with us. While I was out and about, Danita had called me on my cell. I answered as I crept through a major backup on the Baltimore National Parkway, caused by a collision between a Honda Accord and Nissan Pathfinder. The right lane was completely closed off, forcing everyone to have to merge to the left. Damn if everyone and their uncle hadn't been on the road that day.

"Hello?"

"Stephen? Where are you?"

"Hey. You wouldn't believe what has happened over here. I'm still on my way back from DC, but of course, I've run into an accident. The whole right lane is closed off. I've been driving at like ten miles per hour for the past half hour."

"Oh really? So you're nowhere close yet?"

"Nah, afraid not. Everyone's just going to have to wait a little longer for that cobbler you made, which, by the way, I'm anxious to get my hands on."

She laughed. "I hope everyone likes it."

"Baby, if it tastes anything like the peach you give me at night, everyone will love it."

"You are so bad."

"Bad as Michael Jackson and a nose job."

She laughed again. I always did like her laugh. It had been nice to hear that lately as opposed to her growling. "Hey, listen, I have to run to the store for a little while. I was calling to tell you so you'd know where I was. But I'll probably make it back home before you do."

I looked at the time. "Baby, it's almost three o'clock. You know we'll have traffic to deal with. You have to go now?"

"Yes, I do."

"All right, well, I'll see you whenever I get out of this mess."

"Okay, baby. Hurry home. And be careful."

"I will. You do the same."

I hung up the phone with a smile plastered to my face. It felt good as all hell to be back on the smooth road with Danita. For a while, I didn't think we'd get back there.

After another half hour of creeping, the traffic finally started to move again. By the time I got to 295, a whole hour and a half had passed since I had spoken to Danita. As long as it took her to get ready, I was hoping that she would be dressed and ready to go by the time I got home. I called the house, but got no answer. Then I called her cell. Again, I got no answer. I left a message on both the home answering machine and her voice mail, letting her know that I would be home soon.

As I cruised, I remembered that I needed to stop and buy a bottle of wine to take for the occasion. I got in the right lane to exit 29 to go to the liquor store, and as I did, I glanced to the right. It just so happened at that particular moment the law office where Danita worked came into view. For no particular reason, I took an extra long glance over there and when I did, I saw her car parked in the lot next to a Mercedes. Of course my mind wondered what she was doing there, so I grabbed my phone and called her cell again. But again, I got no answer. I didn't leave a message. I never even stopped for a bottle of wine. I wanted to be home when she got there. I was showered and dressed by the time she walked in the door.

"Sorry I took so long," she said, walking over to me and giving me a kiss.

"Where were you?"

"I ran to the store and then stopped at my mother's house. She wanted to talk about some things."

"Oh yeah? That's it? You didn't go anywhere else?"

"No, I didn't. Why?"

"It's just that you were gone so long, I thought you may have made a stop somewhere."

She shrugged her shoulders and kissed me on my cheek. "Nope. No stops."

"I see."

I was about to say more when the phone rang. I picked it up and was greeted by the sound of my mother's yell. "Boy, why are you two not here yet? Don't you know people are over here waiting to eat?"

"I'm sorry, Moms. We got held up." I gave a glance toward Danita, who had moved away and was now in the bathroom. "We're on our way now."

"Okay, but please hurry. You know I'm not trying to start without you. But if you don't get here, these people are going to riot."

"Tell Pops and Kyle to chill. We'll be there."

I hung up the phone and yelled, "They're all waiting for us."

Danita came out of the bathroom with a new application of makeup on her face. I watched her. "Did you get everything you needed from the store?"

She smiled. "No. I didn't."

There was something in the way she said that that made me feel like there was a hidden meaning. I was about to mention my seeing her at her job when the phone rang again.

"Hello?"

"Stephen, make sure that you don't forget the peach cobbler. And will you two please leave!"

I hung up the phone and eyed Danita again. She stared back at me, but it almost felt like she was looking through me.

"My moms said not to forget the cobbler."

"It's ready to go."

We left the apartment then. I had decided to let the issue rest and store it away in the back of my mind. Besides, I wasn't in the mood to argue, or even come close to that. It was New Year's Day, and

I wanted to start it off right. Arguing on the first day would've been a bad omen of things to come, and I didn't want that. It's just too bad that, as I closed the door and locked it, I knew that the bad omen had already come in the form of her lie.

13

Weeks after it had happened, I still couldn't get the fact that Danita had lied to me out of my mind. Questions plagued me like a bad cold that wouldn't go away.

Why had she lied?

What did she have to hide?

What did she have to go to her job for?

Whose car had that been parked next to hers?

On and on, they kept coming, like angry waves. My girl flat-out lied to me, looked me in the eye, and then went about her business. The more I thought about it, the angrier I became, and the more it hurt. But I didn't say anything to her. I decided to watch her movements and see if anything else strange occurred. Who knows, maybe she just needed to pick something up, and it was so unimportant that stopping at her job never really stayed on her mind? Maybe the Benz parked next to hers had been broken down and was left there? Maybe I had nothing to worry about?

I tried to buy into those thoughts, but the more I observed, the more I felt like something was going on. That New Year's Day lie was the first of the bad things to come. As each day passed, we were becoming distant again.

Little by little, I noticed subtle changes in her moods and behavior. She began to move in strange ways. Ways that seemed as if she had something to hide.

She began going out solo with her friends more frequently. At least, that's what she told me. I had my doubts. Especially when she would come home and shower before she climbed in the bed beside me. When I asked her about that, her explanation was, "I wanted to get the smoke scent off of me." I never said anything after that. I just stored things away in my memory, especially how the clothes she had worn and discreetly tried to shove deep into the hamper, never had a smoke scent at all.

Yeah, I checked them.

There were other signs that something was going on.

I watched with a curious eye as she began taking phone calls in another room, which she hadn't done before. And if she wasn't going in another room, she would do strange things like lower the cell volume when she was talking to someone. As each day went by, I watched as she and her phone became joined at the hip.

Unfortunately, with my suspicions rising, I started to feel the need to do some investigating. I wanted to know whom she was talking to, and when. I had to know, just to ease my mind. It may have been the wrong thing to do, but I started to check her phone when I could. Sometimes I'd wait until she was asleep or in the bathroom, then scroll through her incoming and outgoing call history. A few of the numbers I'd seen belonged to her friends, her mother, and a couple from me. But more than half of the calls, I noticed, were either to or from a cell number with no name attached to it. I took note of the times the calls were made, which ranged from as early as 6:00 in the morning to as late as 1:00 in the morning, and then I stored the number away in my memory.

I debated with myself for weeks about calling the number. After all, our relationship had been founded on trust and to call that number would betray everything that our relationship stood for. At least, that's what I told myself. But even as I said that, I knew I had to call. I had to know what was going on. The questions and unknown answers were beating me up daily. There was no other alternative for me. And so I called. From Danita's cell.

"Hey you," a male voice answered.

I hung up without saying anything. The voice was all I needed to hear. After that, I started making subtle comments to Danita whenever her cell phone rang. Saying things like, "What guy do you have calling all the time?" Or, "It's him again." I made so many smart remarks, that eventually Danita got tired of it all, and snapped at me one day.

"Stephen, why is it that when my phone rings, you always assume it's a man?"

I looked at her and smiled inwardly. I could hear the irritation in her voice. I enjoyed that. "Because, Danita, no woman I know calls like that."

"So what, I can't have female friends calling me

like that? I'm getting sick and tired of your comments."

"Hey, if you don't like my comments, just do what you normally do and walk away and take the call somewhere else."

"Oh, so you're checking up on me now?"

"Not checking," I said, watching her. "Just observing. You think I don't see how you go off whenever you get on your phone?"

"So what, you don't trust me?" She put her hand on her hips and craned her neck.

"Should I?"

We stared at each other and then she said, "What do you mean by that? Are you accusing me of something?"

"Is there something to accuse you of? And why are you getting all hyped about it? I was just playing," I lied.

She sucked her teeth. "Playing my ass. You think I don't notice the way you are when my phone rings? You think I don't see how you pay attention when I'm on the phone? I leave the room to get away from all of that."

I nodded my head and bit down on my bottom lip. "I see." I could see her getting more flustered. Damn, she looked guilty.

"I didn't realize me being on the phone was such a problem for you. Why is that?"

I shrugged my shoulders. "I don't know. I guess it's just weird to me that you never used to do that before. But maybe it's just my imagination."

"Oh, it's your imagination, all right. I'll tell you one thing, you better get it in check. Because I refuse to be under a magnifying glass like that."

"What are you tripping about, Danita?"

"I don't like being monitored!"

"Monitored? Who's doing that? I just said it was weird that every time your phone rang, you leave the room to take it."

"Un, huh. I'm not stupid, you know."

"Never said you were."

Danita sucked her teeth again and crossed her arms. "You know what? If you want to act like some non-trusting fool, then maybe you need to do it from somewhere else."

"Isn't that the pot calling the kettle black? But you're right . . . maybe I do," I said seriously. I had been thinking about getting my own place for a while.

"Yeah, maybe you do." Danita walked away then, leaving me with a sense of satisfaction that I had gotten under her skin.

After that argument, my imagination started working double-time. Whenever I would hear her laughing on the phone, I'd wonder whom she was laughing with. Was it the voice with no name? In my head, I started coming up with different conversations she could've been having. When she said, "I can't do that," I imagined that voice saying, "Why don't you come see me?" If she said, "We can do that tomorrow," I imagined him saying, "Let's see each other."

As unhealthy as it was, I started paying more and more attention to every word she was saying when she was on her calls. And I never tried to hide it, which got on her nerves. It didn't matter whom she was talking to. I just listened, and I never said a word, because I didn't have any real proof that anything was going on. Oh, I had strong feelings, and certainly her lies and actions didn't help, but I still hadn't actually seen anything. And that's what I wanted. I wanted to see before I made any moves. I was determined to get the full truth before I put myself out there. I didn't want to give her any opportunity to turn anything back around on me.

After that phone call, the game began, and things were irreversibly changed.

1:00 AM

Diary,

Jeff and I made love for the first time and it was incredible. It was filled with unbelievable passion. It reminded me of the way Stephen and I used to make love in the beginning, when things were good between us. Jeff took his time with me and satisfied my body in a way that it hadn't been in a long time. It had been awhile for me, because Stephen and I had stopped being intimate. So, I had a lot of pent-up energy just waiting to be let loose.

And that's exactly what happened.

We were in his office. We had both stayed late to catch up on some work. Since my promotion from secretary to training paralegal, I had a lot more work to do, and I was really staying there to work. But then Jeff came over to my desk, and without warning, kissed me and started caressing me. We took off from there and made our way, kissing and touching. Eventually, we went back to his office, where we closed the door, locked it, and made love on his executive black leather chair. I rode him while he sucked on my neck and breasts like he hadn't eaten in days. It was intense, and more than I had ever expected.

When we were finished, an unbelievable feeling of guilt came over me. I had to leave right away. Although we'd come extremely close, we'd never actually gone the whole way. I just couldn't bring myself to do it. Anytime we had come close to it, I would back out because Stephen would always pop into my mind. And that was a problem. Because I still loved Stephen with all my heart and I didn't want to lose him.

14

Danita

I finally broke down to Latrice and told her what had been going on between Jeff and me. She'd been hounding me after Emily had told her about the rumors at work, and I really needed to talk to someone. I figured she was the best person to confide in, because I knew she would have my back no matter what.

I was wrong.

"What you mean you and Jeff are sleeping together? You're kidding, right? I know you got to be kidding. Please tell me you're not serious."

My voice was a whisper. "Yes, girl. Jeff and I are seeing each other."

"Seeing each other? Danita, the man is married! And he's your boss! What the hell is wrong with you? And stop staring down at that stain. That's not who's talking to you."

I lifted my head and looked up at my best friend. We had just finished a shopping splurge at the mall, and were sitting in her kitchen, resting our feet and letting our corns breathe, when I had decided to open up.

"I know who's talking to me, okay?" I said, struggling to keep eye contact with her. Her reaction had not been what I expected at all. Of all people, I thought she would have been the one to understand. "You're seeing Bernard, aren't you? I don't think his wife would appreciate that."

"Uh, uh. Don't you even go there with me."

"Why, 'Trice? What's the difference with me and Jeff, and you and Bernard?"

Latrice slammed her hand on the table and sucked her teeth. "What's the difference? Do you even have to ask me that?"

I looked at her hard. I was actually getting angry that she was coming down on me like that. "Yeah, why? What the hell is the difference?"

Latrice stared back at me with a look that could make any man or woman cower. "First of all, Bernard is not my fucking boss. I may do some crazy things, but the last thing I'm going to do is fuck my boss. Have you lost your mind? That is one line you should never, ever cross. I thought you, of all people, had more sense than that. What the hell made you even go there with him?"

I started to answer, but then she cut me off.

"Second of all, Bernard is not Stephen. Girl, Stephen is a good man who loves you to no end. If he knew how, he would flip over backwards for you. Shit, he's already jumped through hoops for your ungrateful ass."

I raised my eyebrows. "Excuse me?"

Latrice curled her lips. "Ungrateful ass. That's what I said. Danita, do you know how hard it is to find a man like Stephen? He's fine, intelligent, and he's the furthest thing from a playa a man could be. Why would you even want to risk losing that? Over what? What do you possibly think you and your boss can have? He's a fucking married man with kids. With kids, Danita! Why are you trying to break up the man's family? And I use that term loosely, because no *real* man would do what he's doing!"

"What makes Bernard a man?" I screamed. I was so angry and hurt by her comments and questions. Truth be told, I was angry at the truth of it all. "He has a daughter."

"Who he hasn't seen in twelve years, who calls another man her daddy! I can't believe you're trying to justify your shit by bringing mine down. Girl, Bernard is getting a divorce. You know this. He and his soon-to-be ex-wife are separated. She knows about us, because Bernard was *man* enough to tell her he didn't love her selfish ass and that he wants to be with me. Bernard loves me, girl. What the hell do you think your boss feels?"

"Latrice, Jeff is not the villain you're making him out to be. He's a good man. He cares about me. He pays attention to me . . . does things for me Stephen doesn't or won't do."

"Are you really that simple, Danita? Stephen loves you. Your boss just wants a little ass on the side, which you obviously oblige him with. How could you even think of doing this to Stephen? How could you lower yourself like this? Damn, Danita! Are you that much of a bitch?"

"Watch yourself, Latrice. You may be my friend, but watch yourself."

"Or what?"

I didn't answer her because I knew my threat

was empty, although I didn't like being called out of my name. Besides, getting in a fight with Latrice wasn't what I had wanted to do. I exhaled and kept my voice low when I spoke again.

"You don't understand. I know Stephen loves me. I love him too. Don't . . . say anything. I do love him. But you don't know what it's been like ever since I found that condom. It's like I can't trust him. I'm scared to. And things have changed. The love has changed." Tears leaked from my eyes and cascaded down my cheeks.

"Danita, you are a real trip. All this time you've been giving Stephen a hard time over that condom and accusing him of cheating on you and look at what you're doing."

"Latrice, this was Stephen's fault. If he wouldn't have—"

"Wouldn't have what? Danita, I'll be straight up with you. I don't think Stephen did anything. And even if he did, the man is so good to you, one slip won't hurt. But he didn't do shit and you know it. Girl, that man loves you. He wouldn't betray you like that."

"How do you know? How the hell do you know? I found the condom."

"It was unopened."

"What the hell are you defending him for, Latrice! I'm supposed to be your friend!"

"I'm defending him because the man truly loves you! And if I wasn't your friend, I would be on your ass, trying to keep you from losing a man that would do anything to make you happy."

"Do you have any idea what finding that condom did to me? Do you have any idea how many bad memories that brought up?"

"Oh please, Danita. I don't want to hear it. You're crying over niggas that didn't mean shit! They fucked up. Stephen didn't! Stop making up damn excuses, Danita. And stop trying to put your nonsense on his shoulders."

"Nonsense?"

"Yes, nonsense. Because that's what this is. You running around with your boss is nonsense. You risking losing the best man you could possibly have is nonsense. You sitting there with your simple-hyp-ocritical-ass tears is nonsense. You make me sick, Danita. What? You think your boss is going to leave his family for your ass? Why? Because he says some bullshit about caring for you? It's because of black women like you that our good black men turn the other way and head for the white or Spanish women." Latrice stood up, went to the sink, and stared out through her window.

"That hurt, Latrice."

"Oh, did it? Well, that's too damn bad. Get up out of my place, Danita. I love you, but I can't back you on this because I am a real friend. I work with Stephen, girl. I like Stephen. I can't look him in the eye knowing that his woman, my *friend*, is sleeping around on his ass."

I kept silent as I watched Latrice to see if she was really serious. She kept her back to me and wouldn't turn around. I shook my head. We'd had fights dur-ing our ten years of friendship before, but never this intense. Neither one of us had ever turned our backs. I didn't want to keep arguing, but what she said wasn't true.

"I'm not sleeping around, Latrice. I care about Jeff."

"And you love Stephen, right?"

"Stephen and I have . . . issues . . ."

"Shut up, Danita. No relationship is without its share of issues. Did you really expect for you and Stephen to never have any?"

"It's not that simple."

"Life isn't simple, Danita. Just filled with simple-ass people who do simple-ass things."

Neither one of us said anything for a few seconds. I stood up and thought about approaching her. I want to stop the fighting. I stared at Latrice's back and took a deep breath and released it slowly. Ten years, I thought. Was that about to end? I opened my mouth to say something but Latrice beat me to it.

"Please grab your shit and leave, Danita. And don't worry, I won't say anything to Stephen. I'll honor our friendship by that much. I'll leave it up to you to do the right thing. Come and check me when and if you do." Without saying another word, Latrice walked out of the kitchen, leaving me standing alone.

I didn't want to go home right away, so I drove around Columbia and then to downtown Baltimore to do some thinking. Was I really doing what Latrice had said I was? Was I really trying to justify my relationship with Jeff by blaming all of this on Stephen and the condom? I parked in the garage under the Hyatt and walked alone with my thoughts to the harbor. I sat and listened to a steel band as they played for a small jubilant crowd.

As I sat, I watched couples walking by holding hands. I saw couples hugging as they sat and listened to the Caribbean melody being played.

Couples.

I thought back to my blind date with Stephen and how we had walked the harbor, just talking for hours. We had clicked so well. It had seemed as though we were made for each other. What happened? Was it really that condom? Or was there something else? Did I really love Stephen like I said I did? How real was what I felt for Jeff? Could I stop it? As I listened to the island tunes, I tried to figure out the answers.

15

Stephen

Before summer had come to an end, I had moved out of the apartment with Danita and gotten my own place. It had been a long time coming. Although we had been living under the same roof and sharing the same bed, we hadn't been together for a while. A lot of things had changed for both us. Our love was fading as each day passed. And the mistrust, especially on my end, was growing. I continued to watch my back and play detective. I felt like I had no choice. I still hadn't been able to figure out who she was seeing, but there was no doubt in my mind that it was somebody. I started to continuously check her cell phone's caller ID, and I would've tried to listen to her voice mails, if I had known her pass code.

"Kid, you playing Dick Tracy is not healthy. Why don't you just end the relationship?"

I was sitting with Carlos at Mi Rancho restaurant in DC. For a Puerto Rican, Carlos loves him some Mexican food. The last time we spoke, I had told him about my suspicions about Danita. As we were scarfing down some steak and chicken fajitas, I told him all that I had discovered in the past couple of months. I had kept it all to myself until then.

"I love her, man. I don't want the relationship to end."

"Bro, if she's fucking around on you, then it's already over. You feel me?"

I nodded my head. "I know, I know. But I haven't confirmed any of it yet. I'm basing my feelings on things I've seen and noticed."

"So confront her about it."

"How? It's not like I can say, 'Hey, you've been fucking around. I know because I've been checking your phone.' Know what I mean?"

"True, true. Bro, if you have to go to those extremes . . . You just need to step away."

"Want to hear something deranged?"

Carlos swallowed some of his *horchata* drink and took a forkful of rice and beans. "What's up?" he said, with his mouth full of the delicious food that I barely had an appetite for.

"It might sound sick, man, but besides loving her and wanting to work everything out, the other reason why I'm still in this is because it's become like a game to me."

"A game? Since when did stressing yourself out become a game?"

"So, I should end this and ease my mind, right?"

"Right."

"Wrong. If I do that, kid, I lose."

"Lose what?"

"Man, if Danita is out there, and I walk away, then she wins, and I'll be the fool."

"You'll be a less-stressed fool, bro."

"I can't have that Carlito. I want . . . no, I *need* to catch her. I need to catch her in the act. I want her to be the fool. I want her to know that while she was gaming me, I was playing my game too, only I won. For all the shit that she'd thrown in my face, making me out to be the son of a bitch, I want her and everyone else to know it was all about her. You feel me?"

Carlos scratched his goatee and nodded his head slowly. "Yeah, I feel you."

"Plus, I want to see who the fuck she's running around with."

"And what happens when you find out who it is? You tryin' to go to jail over her?"

I sat silent for a long minute before I answered, because the truth was, I didn't really know what I would do. I knew the thug in me wanted to kick some ass from Monday to Sunday, but the sensible black man in me didn't want to go to jail—especially over a woman.

But still . . .

"Man, I'm not exactly sure what I'm gonna do."

"Bro . . . too many fools end up losing their lives over pussy."

"I know, man. And I know the right thing to do would be to do nothing, but I can't promise that I won't."

"At least promise me one thing, bro."

"What's that?"

"That before you do, you give me a call first. Cool?"

I nodded. "All right, man. I think I can do that."

"You better, bro."

"All right . . . I will."

Carlos gave me a serious look and then extended his hand to me. As I took it, he said, "Aight, bro. You better make that call first, because I ain't trying to come and see your ass in the pen. I have enough family in there. *Entiendes*?"

I held onto his hand with a firm grip and kept my eyes trained on his. "I understand, man."

With that last statement, Carlos had said all he needed to say—all I needed to hear. He wasn't just my boy. He was my brother.

After that conversation, I did exactly what I said I would—I continued my game. Moving out had been my power play, because it had gotten me away from the daily pressure of saying anything to her about what I knew. The longer I stayed there, the more I wanted to go off. And I didn't want that, because I still had to see who she was seeing. So moving out was just the thing I needed. Plus, I'll be honest, I was also hoping that, somehow, by moving out and not being around her all the time, she would start to miss me. But that didn't happen. As a matter of fact, unless I called her or stopped by to see her, days could go by without us speaking. I called her and asked her about that once.

"Danita, it's been three days since we've spoken. What's up?"

I heard her sigh. "I've been busy, Stephen. You know ever since my promotion, work has been taking up all my time. By the time I get home, I'm so worn out, the only thing I'm able to do is sleep."

"A five-minute phone call wouldn't hurt, you know."

"Stephen, in five minutes' time, I'm off to dreamland. Besides, I haven't heard my phone ringing either."

That's because you're always on it, I wanted to

say. Instead I said, "I haven't tried to call you because I got tired of hearing how you have no time to talk."

"Well, there you go."

"So what, you can't take a few minutes out of your busy day to call your man?" I could feel myself getting angrier.

"Well, I figured my *man* would understand and be patient enough for me to call when I could."

"I understand all about being busy, but damn, a call to say hi goes a long way, you know."

"Look, Stephen, we're talking now, aren't we?"

"Yeah, because *I* called."

"Let's not start anything, please. I've had a long day, and I'm tired."

"Of course you are."

"Damn it, Stephen, what do you want from me? We don't speak for a few days, and you act like it's the end of the world. Grow up."

"Grow up? Me? How about you grow up and start acting like you're in a relationship?"

"Oh please. Just because we don't speak for a couple of days doesn't mean there's no relationship. Get a grip, Stephen. We can't be all up in each other every day. That wouldn't be healthy for either one of us."

"A phone call to say hi? How could that hurt? I mean, damn, we used to live together. How can we go from that to where we are now? Is this relationship not important to you?"

"You know this is important to me. If it wasn't, I wouldn't still be with you. Especially after all that's happened."

I ignored her last comment. "Distancing yourself is a funny way of showing how important I am."

"A little distance is not always a bad thing. Who knows, it may help."

"Right."

"Stephen, I have to go."

"Of course you do."

Nothing changed.

16

Danita

I couldn't believe it had been two months since Latrice and I had spoken. I never expected her to sell me out the way she did. I mean, she may have been Stephen's friend too, but she was my girl. I never would've thought her loyalty would have lay anywhere else but with me.

Bitch.

As many times as I've covered for her triflin' ass, she had the nerve to come down on me like her shit never stank. Well, forget her. If she couldn't be my friend and be in my corner, then I didn't need her. I would be just fine without her. Probably better off anyway. I wouldn't have to deal with her trying to make me feel guilty.

Telling me that I was the one who was wrong. That I was dwelling on nonsense. That I needed to let the past go. What the hell did she know?

She'd really hurt me. I wish I didn't think about her so damn much. Damn her and her honesty.

After Stephen had moved out and gotten his

own apartment, my affair with Jeff really took off. Since I didn't have Stephen around me 24-7, we started seeing more and more of each other. But even though I was happy, I still questioned what we were doing. And as much as I had tried to not let it, the things Latrice had said were getting to me. As each day went by, and Stephen and I spoke less, guilt pressed down harder on my shoulders.

That weight only became heavier the day I met Jeff's wife. She had come by the office to see him. It was the end of the day, and Emily and I were the only paralegals still there. Jeff and I were going to get together that evening because he was leaving for vacation the next day with his family. But Emily had some extra work to take care of, which spoiled that plan. After letting me know that he would stop by my place later, I got ready to leave. As I was heading out the door, Jeff's wife was heading in. I had recognized her from the pictures Jeff had in his office.

"Hello," she said with a friendly smile. "I'm Marion, Jeff's wife. Is he here?"

I smiled back at her as my heart beat heavily. She was even more attractive than the picture showed. She had model features, which hadn't surprised me, as vain as Jeff was. She wore a skirt that hung just above her knees, showing off a pair of extra long legs. Caramel complected, her hair was curly and hung down to the middle of her back. Her eyes were gray, and her body was toned by obvious hours spent at the gym

Oh yeah, I checked her out in thirty seconds flat.

As I prepared to answer her, I heard Jeff's voice behind me.

"Baby? What are you doing here?"

"Hey you," she said, walking past me. "I just came by to say hi." I watched her as she hugged and kissed him lovingly on the very same lips I loved kissing. As he hugged her back, he looked at me and smiled. Then he did something I didn't think he'd do. He called my name as I laid my hand on the doorknob to leave.

"Danita. Don't leave yet. Let me introduce you to my wife."

I turned around slowly and gave him a glare that only he would understand. Then I put on my smile.

"Marion, this is Danita Evans. She's the newest member of our team. She started here a few months ago. Danita, my wife, Marion."

I shook Marion's hand with my cold and sweaty hand. "We've met. But it's nice to meet you again."

"Likewise," she replied.

Damn, she was friendly. I kept my eyes on hers. "Well, I've got to get going. I have a dog at home that I'm sure is going to need an ass-whooping tonight."

Marion laughed and wrapped her arms around Jeff's waist. Before I left, I looked at him and could tell by the look in his eyes that he understood who the dog had been. Then I said, "See you later."

On the drive home, I was pissed. How could Jeff have put me in that predicament? How could he have just stood there and smiled the way he had, as though everything had been fine? I laid into him when he came over to my place that evening. Stephen was out with Carlos, probably hoeing around somewhere, so I knew that he wouldn't be coming by. But to be safe, I parked my car around the corner, by another row of houses, so it looked like I wasn't home, and Stephen didn't have a key.

"You enjoyed seeing your wife and me together today, didn't you?" I had my arms folded across my chest. I was seriously ticked off.

"What makes you ask me that?"

"Because I saw the little smirk on your face that you could barely hide."

"That wasn't a smirk."

"Un, huh. Whatever, asshole. I know what I saw. It was definitely a smirk. And I didn't appreciate that shit."

"Come on, Danita. Everything was cool. Why are you gonna trip over it?"

"Everything was cool? For who?"

"What do you mean?"

I pointed straight at him. "Don't play innocent with me. I saw the look on your face."

"What look?"

"That I'm-the-motherfucking-man look. Like you were the pimp with his hoes standing around him."

"Danita, you're making something out of nothing."

"Whatever, Jeff. I know you got off on that shit. Your wife and your mistress. You men are all the same. Whether it's by cheating or perpetrating like you're the man, you men are always needing to do some shit to have your fucking egos stroked."

Jeff approached me and took my hand in his, and gave me a puppy-dog stare. "Danita, please don't use the word *mistress*. You mean more to me than that. Saying *mistress* is like saying you don't mean much to me. And you mean so much more to me than you know. And whether you believe it or not I wasn't getting off on what happened. I had no idea Marion was going to show up like that. I was caught off guard, and I tried to handle it the best way that I could."

I pulled my hands away and averted my gaze from his. I didn't want to be wooed by him. I was too angry. Mentioning the fact that I was his woman on the side had brought to light, even more, what I hadn't been able to stop thinking about since my blowup with Latrice.

I didn't know what kind of woman his wife was, but I had always wondered how he could see me as much as he did, without her having a problem with it. The only thing I could figure was that either she was naive and had no clue that he was stepping out on her, or she knew he was fooling around, but loved his money so much that she didn't care. After meeting her, I could tell from the gleam in her eyes that she truly loved and trusted him, and that made me feel terrible and ugly inside.

"What's wrong?" he asked me softly.

I turned my back to him and folded my arms across my chest. The night wasn't supposed to go that way. He was going to be away for three weeks. We were supposed to have been wrapped in each other's arms that night, savoring our moment and time spent together. But as badly as I had wanted to, I couldn't deny that I wasn't only disrespecting myself, I was disrespecting Jeff's family.

"Talk to me, Danita," Jeff persisted.

I didn't say anything to him right away because random thoughts were flooding my mind.

Thoughts of Latrice and her comments to me.

Thoughts of Stephen and his love.

Thoughts of my mother. What would she say if she knew?

What did I really think?

I wanted them to all go away. I wanted to be naked in Jeff's capable arms. But instead of doing that, I found myself wiping away a tear from the corner of my eye, and before I could keep my thoughts from becoming words, I asked, "Do you love your wife, Jeff?"

I could hear him sigh behind me. "Why would you ask me that?"

"It's a simple question, Jeff. Do you love your wife?"

"Danita, you know how I feel about you."

"Not me, Jeff. Your wife. Do you love her?"

"What do you want to hear?"

"The truth."

Jeff sighed. "Yes, I love her."

"And your children? Do you love them too?"

"What kind of a question is that? Of course I do."

I squeezed my eyes tightly shut and shook my head. "This is wrong. What we're doing is wrong."

"Danita . . . don't say that. What we have is a good thing. Good for both of us."

"No, it's not, Jeff. It could never be good for both of us."

"Danita . . ."

"Jeff, if you love her, then why are you here with me?"

"I care about you. You know that."

"But you love your wife."

He cracked his knuckles and then approached me and wrapped his arms around me and kissed my shoulder. "Why are you talking about this now, Danita? Don't you love what we have together?"

I pushed away from him. "You and I don't have anything. We work together, and we fuck."

"Come on, baby. We have more than that, and you know it."

"What? What the hell do we have?"

He reached out for me. "Let's not do this now, all right?" I backed away and put my hands up, letting him know not to touch me. He frowned. "Danita, I'm going to be gone for three weeks. Let's let our bodies do the talking right now." He tried to reach out for me again, and again I held him at bay. He sighed. "Danita, I don't want this night to be like this."

"I didn't want it to be like this either, but today got to me. I shook your wife's hand, and I smiled in her face like my shit didn't stink. Jeff, I'm fucking you. I would kill a bitch if she disrespected me like that."

"So, what are you saying?"

"I'm saying that what we're doing isn't right. And the worst part is as each day that passes, I find myself caring about you more and more. And that's sad."

"How is that sad? I care about you too."

"But you're never going to leave her, which means I'll only ever be the trick on the side. You have your cake in Marion, and you're eating it with me. I can't have that anymore."

"Danita—"

I cut him off before he could say another word. I needed to finish what I'd started while I had the strength to do it. "We need to stop seeing each other."

"Danita, don't say that."

"I just did. We can't go on like this. It's not fair to the ones we say we love, and it's not fair to either one of us."

"Can't we talk about this?"

"We just did."

"So it's like that? We just go back to being strictly business? It's that easy for you?"

"It's like that," I said bluntly. I could feel the tears welling in my eyes. I didn't want him to see me crying. I didn't want him to see just how much he had gotten to me. "Leave, please," I whispered.

The room was filled with nothing but silence for a good long minute. I didn't want to say the things I had said, but I knew I had to. Latrice had been right. It may have hurt when she'd said it, but the reality was that I had lowered myself. Suddenly, the risk of losing Stephen didn't seem worth taking anymore.

"Leave, Jeff," I said again.

No longer caring, I let the tears cascade down across my cheeks. I didn't turn around as the front door open and closed softly.

17

Stephen

I didn't want to believe what I saw.
I *tried* not to believe it.

I opened and closed my eyes a couple of times, just hoping that I was dreaming—praying that I hadn't really seen him walk into Danita's place.

I stood in the shadows and waited and watched and fumed. I was burning up. All of my suspicions and doubts and fears had been confirmed. Now, I was through with her shit and being disrespected. I was two steps away from storming up to her front door and kicking it in with the Lugz I was wearing, and administering an ass-whooping neither of them would ever forget when her front door opened and the brother, who'd been wearing a pair of jeans and white T-shirt, walked out. A half hour had passed, which had only made me more heated, because that had been just enough time for a quickie.

I paced and debated. I thought about Carlos and his desire to not come visit me in jail. I thought about the promise I'd made. I thought about the impact whatever action I decided to take would have.

In a matter of seconds I did a lot of thinking.

And then I said *fuck it.*

No more thoughts.

I rushed him.

He was about to open the door to his Benz and get in, when I barreled into his back and sent him crashing forward against it. "You want to fuck with another man's woman, motherfucker!" I yelled, pummeling him with several body blows the likes of which I'd administered to Carlos's body bag, before tossing him to the ground. "You want to fuck with my woman!" I yelled, kicking him viciously in his midsection.

Some would say that it hadn't been a fair fight because I'd attacked him from behind. That it had been cowardly on my part. I'd argue that it was only fair considering that he was fucking with my woman. I knelt down beside him as he struggled to gather himself and stand up, and punched him in his face two times. "You want to fuck with my woman!"

"Oh my God! Stephen!"

Suddenly, Danita's arms were wrapped around my neck.

"Stephen! No! Stop!" she screamed, trying to pull me back.

"You fucking bitch!" I yelled, prying her arms from around me. "You fucking bitch! All the shit you put me through!" I pushed her back and then turned back to her lover. He was still on the ground, moaning. "This is what happens when you fuck with another man's woman, motherfucker!" I kicked him again in his midsection.

Behind me, Danita begged for me to stop again. I turned and stared at her through bloodshot eyes.

"I never did shit to you, Danita! You hear me, bitch? I was never unfaithful to you!"

Danita cried heavily. She reached an arm out toward me and said, "I know, Stephen. I . . . I'm sorry. Please . . . please don't—stop!"

I let out a guttural scream and turned back to the man I'd never seen before. I was about to attack him again when I saw something in the window of his car. It was a man with a twisted face of rage, and eyes filled with murder. His hands were balled into tight fists, ready to inflict pain. For some reason, he looked familiar to me. Like someone I recognized. The hair—curly. The goatee—faded. The eyes—though laced with venom, were small, slightly slanted.

My reflection.

I shook my head and stared.

Danita called my name from somewhere far away.

The man I didn't know moaned again.

I stared at my reflection. Said to myself that my eyes had been playing tricks on me. That it couldn't have been me I was seeing. That I hadn't lost control that way.

Danita screamed my name.

I turned and looked at her.

She was crying. Begging for me to stop. Begging me to forgive her.

I shook my head. "I . . . I loved you," I said. "I fucking loved you."

"I . . . I know. I'm so sorry. Please . . . please stop. Please forgive me."

I looked at her. Then looked to him. The man I

wanted to kill. I looked at my reflection in his car window again and hated what I saw.

I shook my head and then let my fists go slowly. I turned and looked at Danita one last time. And then I walked away, leaving Danita on the ground in the satin robe I'd bought for her.

"What's up, bro?" Carlos said, answering the phone.

"I caught her," I said softly. I was sitting in the driver's seat of my car.

"Caught who, bro?"

"Danita."

"You mean caught, caught? Like with her ass sticking in the air?"

"May as well have been," I said, squeezing the steering wheel. "The motherfucker walked out of her place."

"It could be an innocent thing?"

"Kid, he was driving the same Benz I saw on New Year's."

"Maybe he was dropping somethin' off from work."

"She was dressed in nothing but a fuckin' satin robe that I bought for her."

"Word?"

"Yeah."

"Damn.

"Bro . . . tell me you didn't do anything. Tell me that you stuck to your promise and called me first."

And why the fuck was her car not around and all her lights off, like she wasn't home?"

I didn't answer him right away.

Carlos said, "Bro?"

"Sorry, man, but I can't tell you that," I said, thinking about the blows I'd given.

"Damn," Carlos whispered. "Where are you now?"

"I'm sitting in the car right now."

I heard Carlos give a sigh of relief. "Are they still alive?"

I know the question had been a serious one, but it made me smile. "Yeah. They're breathing."

Carlos let out another sigh of relief. "Head back over here, bro. Can you do that for me?"

My hands were shaking.

"Yeah. I can do that."

"Good. Twenty minutes. I'll look for you in twenty minutes, bro. All right?"

I nodded, strangled the steering wheel again, and said, "All right, man." I ended the call and then started the truck. Before pulling away, I looked across the street and watched Danita help that son of a bitch to his feet.

People always say that when you go looking, you find things you never wanted to see. Despite the obvious signs, I had hoped that wouldn't be the case with Danita. Deep down inside, though, I always knew that the contents of Pandora's box were going to be ugly.

Reality hit me harder than I thought it would. What I didn't know wouldn't hurt me. Well, now I knew.

I pulled off and in the rearview mirror, watched Danita help him inside.

18

Stephen

"You okay?"

I touched my hands, which I'd been soaking in a bowl filled with ice and water, and sighed. "Nah, man. I'm hurting bad."

Carlos nodded and put a hand on my shoulder. "I'm glad you didn't kill anyone, bro."

"Believe me, Carlito . . . I wanted to."

Carlos shook his head. "Well, thank you for not doing that."

He gave me a smile. I gave him a half one back.

"I should have followed your advice and done my thing."

"Nah. That only works when you're a super-pimp like me, bro. You did the right thing."

"Damn, man. Whenever she needed me, I was there. Whenever she called, I answered. Didn't matter the time or the day. She seriously had all of me."

"You were good to her, no doubt."

"I've been through heartbreak before, but this really hurts, man. She played me bad. Had me running around like a fool in love, while she played the field."

Carlos sat down beside me. "Don't sweat it, bro. There are other *mujeres* out there. The right one."

"Yeah, I know."

"So . . . how bad did you hurt this guy?"

"I don't know. Pretty bad, I think. I wasn't myself at that time, you know."

"Think he'll come after you?"

I shrugged. "I have no idea."

"What if he does?"

I shrugged again. "Guess I'll just have to deal with it if that does happen. I'm calm now, but for his sake, he should stay away from me."

"You mean for your sake, bro."

"Yeah . . . maybe."

I winced as my knuckles throbbed. My reflection had really scared me. Not since I was in my late teens had I lost it that way.

Carlos put a hand on the back of my neck. "Hey, believe it or not, there is a bright side to all of this."

"Yeah? What's that?"

"You didn't buy the ring."

I laughed. He'd had a point. But damn, did it sting. Danita had all I wanted in a woman. She brought light to the darkest of days. She made me smile without even trying. When I asked God to send me a beautiful woman, who could not only be my lover, but my friend, he had sent me Danita. If possible, I would've married her in a heartbeat. Oftentimes, I had imagined us walking down that aisle together, after sealing our bond with a kiss, and then whisking away on our honeymoon, only to come back and eventually start a family. Then years after that, our family would have families of their own, while we grew old together and remained forever in love. I was ready for it all. I wanted to go to sleep and wake up with no one else but Danita by my side. As I sat there, wincing, I accepted the fact that the dream was over.

"I feel you," I said.

"Aight then, bro. So in lieu of that, you can only mope over her for a couple of days."

"Man, I feel you, but I might need more than a couple. I'm not as strong as you."

"Strong? Who said I was strong? Shit, I stay away from relationships to avoid from going through what you're going through right now. Nah, bro. Strong is what you are. And believe it . . . Danita ain't the one for you."

"Thanks, man. I appreciate that."

"It's all good, my brother."

"Thanks also for not getting on me for breaking my promise and not calling you first."

"No need to thank me, bro. I wouldn't have called either, and unlike you, the only thing I'd probably need to ice right now would be a baseball bat, because I most certainly would have taken it with me."

I looked at Carlos.

He looked at me.

He was serious.

I spent the next few hours icing my hand and thinking about a life without Danita in it.

19

Danita

10:00 PM

Diary,
   I'm stressed. Nothing in my life seems to be going right for me right now. Since the night of Stephen's attack on Jeff, things have just been turned upside down for me. God, I can't believe it even happened. I'd seen Stephen angry before, but the rage I witnessed in him that night scared me. There'd been so much pain in his eyes. So much hurt in his voice. I realized right then and there how badly I'd screwed up. The condom had never been his. He'd never been unfaithful. He never deserved to be treated the way I'd treated him. He never deserved to be placed in the same categories as the men before him.
   I am such a fool.
   I lost the best thing in my life over a man that really didn't give a shit about me. Pathetic.
   To keep his marriage intact, Jeff told everyone that he was beaten and robbed. He even went so far

as to get rid of his ATM and credit cards just so that he'd have to order new ones. He barely speaks to me now, which is just fine with me, because I'm over him. I wasted so much time and energy. In a lot of ways, I did far more damage than my any of my exes could have done. With them, the worst wound I received had been a broken heart. But despite their actions, my heart was always able to have been repaired. By screwing around with Jeff, I haven't just given myself a broken heart, I've actually made it disappear. I've called Stephen repeatedly and have even gone by his apartment, hoping that he would talk to me, but he never answers when I call, and he never comes to the door. For all intents and purposes, Stephen is gone. Funny that I could hurt myself more than any man could.

20

Danita

After failing to reach Stephen by phone, e-mail or house visit, I broke down and called Latrice. It was the first time we had spoken in a little over four months, so I wasn't expecting a warm reaction when she answered the phone.

"E-Systems, Latrice speaking."

"Hey girl," I said in a whimper of a voice.

A few seconds of silence passed before Latrice finally responded. "Danita?"

"Yeah girl, it's me." I imagined her lips curling into a frown, and by the chilly tone in her voice, I was sure that's what she was doing.

"What do you want, Danita?"

"To talk. I've missed you."

"Is that so?" she said curtly.

"Yes. I owe you an apology, 'Trice. A big one."

"Hmmph."

I took a deep breath. I knew that calling her wasn't going to be easy.

"Look, Latrice, I understand why you came down

on me the way you did. You were right . . . what I was doing had been wrong and selfish."

"And stupid," Latrice added.

"Yeah. That too. It was just that I couldn't get past having found that condom. Girl, you know I've been hurt before. Stephen wasn't the only man I've given my heart to. "

"He was just the best man."

"Yes, he was. And that's why, when I found the condom, it got to me so bad. When I felt like he had betrayed me, it just threw everything out of whack for me. All of the negative energy that had taken so long to go away came right back."

"Danita, it came back because you let it."

"I know, girl. Believe me. I know."

"You should've trusted Stephen. You should've believed in what you two had built together."

Tears welled in my eyes and cascaded slowly down my cheeks. Latrice had been so right. I should've trusted my man. I should've believed the things he'd said, especially since he'd never given me room to doubt him before.

"I know," I whispered.

"You still sleeping with your boss?"

"No."

"What happened?"

"I woke up."

"About time."

" 'Trice . . . have you seen Stephen today?"

"Stephen? Girl, when was the last time you spoke to him?"

"Four weeks ago. I've been trying to reach him, but some things happened, and since then, I haven't been able to."

Latrice sighed into the phone. "Girl, I don't

know how to tell you this, but . . . Stephen quit E-Systems four weeks ago, and then moved to another state."

My heart stopped beating momentarily. "What?"

"He came in one day, grabbed his things, and handed in his letter of resignation, and walked out."

"What? Quit? Moved? I don't understand. How did you find out?"

"Before he left, he stopped by my desk to say good-bye and to tell me he was moving. Then he gave me all the pictures he had of you. Girl, I never told him we weren't talking. I assumed you guys had broken up. So you had no idea at all?"

"No," I barely got out. "I didn't. Do you know where he went?"

"No. He never said. Girl, what the hell happened between you two?"

I told her all about the fight outside of my house—well the beat down Stephen administered—and then told her about the change between Jeff and me since then.

When I finished, Latrice whispered, "Dayum."

Thankfully she didn't say that she'd told me so.

"Are you sure he didn't mention where he was going? Or what new company he was going to?"

"No. He just handed me the pictures, gave me a hug, and said it was time for him to move on. I asked him where he was going, but he wouldn't tell me."

"Are you sure, Latrice?" I said as a frog formed in my throat.

"I'm sure, girl" Latrice said, her voice subdued.

I dropped the phone and cried heavy tears. Stephen was gone. I'd lost him.

21

Danita

With Stephen having disappeared, I was a wreck. Although four weeks had passed, I still tried calling him over and over on his cell, until I couldn't do that anymore because his number had been disconnected. I went to Carlos's place once to try and pry some information from him, but of course he wasn't trying to have anything to do with me. I even tried his parents, hoping that because of the good relationship I'd had with them, I'd be able to get some information. My call to them didn't go over well.

"I can't believe you have the nerve to call here looking for my son after what you did," his mother had snapped at me.

As close as he was to his family, I really should have expected them to know what had happened, but I still held out hope that Stephen hadn't told them anything. "Mrs. Maxwell, believe me, I am very sorry for what's happened."

"Sorry isn't good enough, Danita. Do you know what you've put my baby through?"

I tried but couldn't hold back my tears as his mother lashed out at me. "I just want to talk to him," I said, sobbing. "I just want a chance to explain."

"Explain what, Danita? Do you have any idea how bad you hurt my son with your disrespect and your lies? What kind of explanation could you possibly give that would make a difference?"

I wiped tears away from my eyes with the back of my hand. "I made a mistake, Mrs. Maxwell. I'm not perfect. Please . . . just tell me how I can reach him. All I want to do is talk to him."

"I think you've done enough already!" she snapped. "Do Stephen and all of us a favor and don't call here anymore."

The line went dead after that, as Mrs. Maxwell hung up on me. I broke down and cried rivers. I couldn't remember ever feeling any worse than I did at that moment. I refused to give up, though, and I tried calling them again a couple of days later. I prepared myself for another verbal war with Mrs. Maxwell, but thankfully, it was Stephen's father who answered this time. I figured my chances at getting in contact with Stephen would be slightly better with him.

I was wrong.

"What do you want, Danita?" he asked callously.

"Mr. Maxwell . . . Can you please tell me how to get in contact with Stephen?"

"I don't think that's a good idea."

"Mr. Maxwell, please . . . all I want is a chance to talk to him. I just want to explain why I made the mistakes I made. Please, Mr. Maxwell . . . I love him." I bowed my head and waited for his response. I'd said all that I could.

"Danita," his father finally said after a long five seconds. "Stephen doesn't want to have anything to do with you right now. Don't call here anymore." And then he too hung up on me.

Losing the respect and friendship from Stephen's parents hurt, because I'd loved them both dearly. I had always envisioned having children and taking them over to their house to be pampered and adored. Now that would never happen. I saw his brother at the mall once, but upon seeing me, he turned and gave me his back as he walked away.

I spent many sleepless nights thinking about Stephen and wondering what and how he was doing. I played love songs alone in the dark and asked myself if he was thinking about me. My unanswered calls and empty answering machine gave me my answer.

I was miserable without Stephen, and it had started to show. I gained a few extra pounds because I stopped going to the gym. Of course, the weight had all settled in my ass and hips. My work performance began to suffer, and Jeff, who had become completely cold to me, was losing his patience. At one point, I had heard rumors of him looking for someone to replace me. But I wasn't having that. One evening, in just a few words, I made sure that the rumors ended the next day.

"Don't make me have another conversation with Marion, Jeff. I have nothing to lose."

And I didn't.

I was already frustrated with my life. Telling his

wife what type of man he really had been wasn't going to hurt me any more than I had already been hurting.

The only constant things in my life, which were bringing a semblance of a smile to my always-frowning face, were my friendships with Latrice and Emily.

After my call to Latrice, we started speaking again. I had made my mistake and paid for it with Stephen's departure. She knew that, and we moved on. Besides, we were family. And as close-knit as we were, we couldn't afford to stay apart for too long.

My relationship with Emily too made a change for the better. We started speaking and taking lunch breaks at work together again. It was at lunch one day when she told me something that made what I had done to Stephen even worse. We were eating at the Tomato Palace by the lake across from the mall when she said, "I slept with Jeff over two years ago."

I stared at her, unable to say a word.

"It was a couple of months after I had started. I was young and naïve. He was handsome, had money, and knew how to use the wordplay. I mean, shit, he is a lawyer, right? I was just a white girl that he wanted to conquer. He fed me his lines, which I believed to be true. And after he got his, it was back to business as usual. He also slept with Jai."

I didn't say a word. Just nodded my head.

"We all got played. I slept with Jeff because I was stupid and he was smooth. Jai slept with him because she's a nasty ho. Why did you sleep with him?"

I remained silent for a second or two, and digested the things she'd told me. Jeff had played me, just like he had them. I was no more special to him than they had been.

"I was stupid too," I admitted solemnly.

"Do you know why I stopped talking to you?"

"I didn't know something had gone on between you two."

"Shit, is that why you think I stopped hanging with you? Oh, hell no. I made my mistake, but I learned my lesson. I stopped talking to you because I was angry that you were letting yourself get played when you already had a fine man. A real man. Me . . . I didn't have anybody special. If I had, Jeff would never have gotten to me. When I took you outside that day and asked you about what I knew was the truth, I was hoping you would have been up-front with me. But you weren't. And then you questioned my friendship with you. At that point, I decided I was going to let the truth burn you like it had me."

I remained stone quiet as the other diners in the restaurant ate, laughed, and conversed. I couldn't say anything. She'd been right to do what she had done. I fucked up. Damn, it was hard hearing the truth.

"I'm sorry," I finally said. "Girl, I wasn't thinking straight."

"You can say that again."

"Em, thank you for letting me fall flat on my face. If you and Latrice hadn't done the things you did, I may have never woken up."

"That's what friends are for. It's just too bad you lost Stephen in the process. Have you heard from him?"

"No."

Emily took my hand. I was starting to cry. I had been doing a lot of that.

"Life goes on, Danita. You'll find another Stephen."

"No," I said with my eyes closed. "I won't. He can't be replaced."

Emily squeezed my hand softly. She knew I was right. I couldn't stop thinking about what I had done and lost. I let the best thing in my life slip right through my fingers. And now I was left alone. I ate the rest of my food in silence, and didn't say another word until we were walking back to our cars.

"Emily, I have to ask you something. I know how I do it, but I'm curious—what do you do to keep Jeff in check?"

Emily smiled and brushed her hand through her cornrowed hair. In her best ghettofied white-girl accent, she said, "Please. I memorized that brother's home number."

I laughed.

I had too.

22

Stephen

The decision to move hadn't been a spur-of-the-moment decision for me. I had been planning it for months. I just hadn't told anyone. Not even Carlos. I didn't want to give him, or anyone, the opportunity to try and talk me out of anything. For the better part of the year, I had been weighing the pros and cons of moving. It wasn't an easy decision to make. I had wrestled with the fact that I would be leaving everything that I had established behind. Friends, family, my good-paying job, which I had been feeling more and more insecure about with all of the layoffs happening.

But after my confrontation with Danita and her lover, the time to leave just seemed the right thing. That chapter was over and the time had come for me to begin a new one.

So a few months ago before all of the shit happened, I began sending my résumé out to different companies. Location didn't really matter to me, although I was leaning toward the Florida sun and beach, and after an interview with ITC Delta-com in Jacksonville, the sun and beach became re-ality.

I accepted their offer as a technical consultant III and started a week after I quit E-Systems. I didn't even bother to give two weeks' notice. I accepted the offer, hopped on my laptop, typed up my res-ignation letter, and then took that and a box to E-Systems. It felt good to walk out on my own rather than being escorted out because of company down-sizing.

Saying good-bye to Latrice hadn't been easy. She and I had become good friends. If she and Danita weren't so close, we'd still be close.

After saying good-bye to her, I called Carlos. Telling him of my decision had been damn hard for me to do. We weren't just friends, we were brothers for life.

"What's up, bro?" he said, giving me a pound. We'd met at Dave and Buster's in Glen Burnie to watch the Monday night football game.

Quick and painless was how I decided to handle it. There was no point in dragging anything out. "Man, I'm leaving."

Confusion in his eyes, Carlos said, "Leaving? Leaving where?"

"I took a job with ITC in Florida. I start next week. But I'm leaving tomorrow."

Carlos looked at me and then at the big screen. His face was somber when he looked back to me. "Damn, bro. Never saw this coming."

"I know, man. I just need a fresh start, you know? I need some new memories. And I need to be in a new place where I can create them."

"I feel you."

"Cool. You okay with it?"

Carlos nodded. "Come on, bro. I ain't your girl. You gotta do what you gotta do. I understand that. What I don't understand is how you could tell me last minute like this. I mean, tomorrow? Bro, you didn't even give me a chance to give you a proper send-off."

I smiled. "Don't worry, kid. You can make up for it when you come to Florida to hang."

Carlos rubbed his palms together, and with a mischievous smile said, "Hell yeah, bro. I'll definitely be hanging down there. South Beach, baby!"

We laughed and gave each other a pound and then grew silent and went back to watching the game.

A few minutes later, Carlos said, "So tomorrow, huh?"

"Yeah."

"You packed?"

"Yeah. I got everything I need. The company's going to be moving my things. I just have to drive down and take the bare essentials with me."

"Damn, kid. You got it like that?"

"They wanted a brother."

"Handle yours, bro."

We ordered two beers and toasted to new beginnings and fine honeys on the beach.

23

Stephen

My first month in Jacksonville was as lonely a month as I could ever remember. I had no friends, save the few acquaintances from work. To pass the time, I spent my days going to the gym to get my workout on. When I wasn't doing that, I was relaxing at my place, just a few minutes away from the beach. ITC had done me right. Set me up in the Avenue Royale with a spacious two-bedroom apartment, decked with a sunroom, home office, and a view of the lake. I couldn't complain at all.

"Kid, the apartment is nice!" I just had to call Carlos and tell him about it after I had moved in.

"Word? You mean it's better than the hotel you were staying at?" Carlos quipped.

"Kid, it is sweet. Check it, I have a sunroom, a home office, a view of the lake."

"Lake? You have a lake there?"

"Kid, I live in the Avenue *Royale*."

"Oh, so you just rulin', huh?"

"You know it."

"What about the sights? Are there any around there? You have two bedrooms, so you know I'ma be tryin' to meet some neighbors."

"Yo, the ladies around here are fwine. Emphasis on the *W*."

"You meet any yet?"

"Not yet, man. I just moved in."

"Man, I would've had a welcoming committee at my door."

"Hey, I've been out of the game for a while. Give me a minute."

"Yeah, yeah rusty."

I laughed. "So, when are you coming down?"

"I'll be there soon, bro. I just have some shit going on at work. I'll look at my calendar and let you know."

"Aight, man. But don't take too long. I don't want to scoop up all the honeys before you get here."

"Bro, please. Scoop up all you want. I don't mind sloppy seconds."

I couldn't contain my laughter. "Aight, man, check that calendar."

"Will do. Holla."

"Peace."

After October breezed by, Thanksgiving arrived with all the speed of a turtle. I didn't have vacation time yet, so I convinced my family to come and visit me. I figured it was a chance for them to come to Florida for some November warmth. When I picked them up from the airport, my moms hugged me as if I'd been kidnapped and gone for years. I hadn't been home since I'd left, and seeing them made me realize just how much I had missed them. My pops and I shared a typical father-son hug, but in his grip I felt how much he'd missed me too. My brother, going through his whole "cool phase," gave me a pound and a shoulder-to-shoulder hug, and said, " 'Sup, bitch!"

"Not much, trick."

We laughed and then shared a real hug. It felt good to have them there. During their visit, I made sure to take each one of them to the places they liked the best.

On the first day, we went out as a whole unit, and I gave them the tour of Jacksonville. Since moving there, the one thing I had made sure to do was become familiar with my new territory. There's nothing like being lost and not knowing a soul.

I took them first to Jacksonville Landing and let them scour through all of the different shops. I pointed out the water taxis by the ocean.

"You know, if we take one of those taxis, we could be at the football stadium in five minutes."

"For real? So when the Ravens come to play the Jaguars, you're getting us tickets, right?" Kyle was a huge football fan like I was.

"Yeah," I laughed. "I got you. As long as your broke ass can pay for the ticket."

"Pops got me. Right, Pops?"

My father smiled. "Pops was never invited into this conversation, and therefore, he cannot hear a word that's being said."

We all busted out laughing. After showing them a few more sights, we stopped into one of the numerous restaurants and ate seafood until we burst. We went home to rest, and that night I treated them all to the Comedy Zone. So far, in day one alone, I had taken care of two birds with one stone: took my mother shopping and took my father to see some comedy, which he loved. That night, while my parents slept in the extra bedroom, Kyle and I chilled and watched TV. We both fell asleep on the couch.

I took care of his desires the next night. He and I went to T-Birds nightclub, where we chilled and enjoyed the different shades and flavors we saw in miniskirts and booty shorts. I had been anxious to be out with my brother. As kids growing up, he and I weren't that close. Because of the age difference, I had never wanted him around much—didn't want him cramping my style. But as he'd gotten older and matured, we became very close. I looked out for him and made sure he stayed on the path he needed to be on. I wasn't trying to have a little brother out there doing nonsense, and he knew that. But I never really had much to worry about with him anyway, because he always had his head on straight. Besides, if it hadn't been, my parents and I would've twisted it back into place.

The rest of the holiday weekend went by in a blur. My mother cooked the Thanksgiving dinner at my place. As usual, she pulled out all the stops. Didn't matter where she was, all she needed was a kitchen. I even offered to help, but the kitchen being her sanctuary, she kicked me out and wouldn't allow me to even cross the threshold.

During their last night there, while my mother slept and my brother watched TV, my pops and I went for a drive. He wanted to "enjoy Jacksonville one more time."

I knew he wanted to talk. We stopped at a small bar and went inside to have a beer. As the waitress walked away, having brought our drinks, my pops looked at me, and in a very low and fatherly voice, said, "How are you holding up, son?"

I knew where he was going with his question. "I'm cool."

"Are you really? I know what went down with you and Danita hit you hard. You know you can't hide that from me. It's okay to hurt, son. Just means you loved with all your heart, which is what we're supposed to do. Forget anyone that says we shouldn't."

I sighed. "She hurt me bad, Pops," I finally admitted. "It's taking a while, but I'll get past it."

"That's what I like to hear. Some people can't or don't do that. Some people just let things sit inside of them and fester until they eventually come out and affect their future. They fail to let things that happen in the past become a memory."

I raised my eyebrow and thought about Danita. "You couldn't be more right," I said.

"So . . . are there any women on the horizon?"

I shook my head. "Nah. Not yet. I'm just chilling, really."

"Nothing wrong with that. Just make sure that when the time comes, and you do get involved, that you give whoever it is all of you. Because, son, that's the only way to do it. Love and hope that you get the same in return. Losing you was Danita's loss. And believe me, she knows that."

"Yeah. I know."

"You're a good man, Stephen. Your mother and I raised you right."

I smiled. "Yeah, you did. But you royally screwed up with Kyle."

My pops smiled. "Yeah, we did."

We laughed. We had a couple of more beers, and then after a game of pool, went back to my place.

When my family left, the void that they filled

opened right up again. It wouldn't close again until I visited for Christmas. I didn't stay in Maryland long, though. I stayed just for the holiday. I didn't see Carlos because he was in New York with his family, so I hung out with Kyle on Christmas eve, opened presents with everyone on Christmas day, and flew back to Jacksonville just before New Year's eve.

For New Year's, Carlos came to visit me. Once he stepped off the plane, the amount of time that had passed since we'd last seen each other became unimportant. It was back to old times, and all bets were off.

"My dog is here!"

"What uuuuuuuuup!" he said, giving me a pound and hug.

"Nothing, kid. Just glad to see you finally got your ass off the couch and came down."

"Man. She was riding me so good I couldn't leave that couch."

"Yeah, aight."

We laughed it up and headed back to my place, where we wasted no time in getting dressed and then hitting the town. We went first to the one spot I knew he would love.

"The New Solid Gold strip club! Ah shit, you know what I want to see!"

"Yeah, kid. I knew your horny ass would be happy with this for our first stop."

"Not horny, dude. Hungry."

"Well, there's plenty to eat here in J'ville."

Carlos looked at me with a constipated glare. "But do you think it's enough to fill the abyss in my loins?" He busted out laughing and so did I. Damn, I had missed him.

We hung out and enjoyed all the jiggling and gyrating the club had to offer. Then, when we were through coughing up dollars for no change, I took him to the T-Birds nightclub. It was even more packed than when I had gone with Kyle.

"Damn, New Year's is the shit down here. Mad girlies in here, man."

"True indeed," I said.

And they really were. Girls outnumbered the guys, which was no problem for two pimps like Carlos and me. We partied the night away in T-Birds, and when it was over, we had four numbers apiece.

Later that night, we went to a slamming party at yet another club. We met up with two of the girls we had met at T-Birds. When the festivities were over, we all headed back to my apartment to ring in the new year the right way.

Carlos's visit was just the thing I needed to ensure that my new year begin the right way. His antics and spirit had been just what I needed. I hadn't laughed like that in a long time. He was my brother for life. I was sad to see him leave when he did, but we made sure that our time apart wouldn't be so long.

In January, I started hanging out with one of the girls I had met on New Year's. Mariana Alonso. A fine, petite *Puertoriquena* with a body so hot she made me sweat when I was near her. When we met, we clicked almost instantly. We both had the same interests—food, movies, TV shows, music, and sports. As an added bonus, like me, she was a Baltimore Ravens fan.

We started hanging out occasionally, meeting for drinks after work or going to the city park, where we'd sit and talk until it got cooler and the sun went down. The more time I spent with Mariana, the more I didn't want our time together to end. We spent late nights on the phone, just talking and getting to know each other more. I found myself daydreaming at work about her smile, and as much as I tried not to let it happen, I found her engulfing my every thought.

Not only was she beautiful, she was also intelligent. She was a credit analyst for one of Jacksonville's largest banks, owned her own condo, drove a convertible Mitsubishi Spider, and refused to let me pay when we went out sometimes—a very smart woman.

For the Super Bowl, we went to her *familia's* house. There, I met her parents, who were on the same level of coolness as my own, her two older sisters, who were equally as fine, and her younger brother, by a year. When she had introduced me to him, he gave me a serious inspection, then smiled and shook my hand. I guess I passed. I also met her uncle, his wife, and their twin ten-year-old daughters, who looked at me with doll eyes and giggled when I smiled at them.

After the game ended and the Colts had won the Super Bowl, more people came over, and as they played some banging salsa, I helped her uncle and father move couches and chairs out of the way and turn the living room into a miniature dance floor. As we danced, Mariana looked at me with her feline eyes and smiled.

"I'm glad you came to Jacksonville, *papi*," she said in my ear as we moved to some *bachata*.

I looked at her and smiled. "So am I," I said.

Then I spun her around, prompting an, *"Aye, papi!"*

She went home with me that night.

Danita never once crossed my mind.

As February rolled around, I had started to realize that I was falling head over heels for Mariana. I loved everything about her. Her smile, her personality, and her sharp sense of humor. And I couldn't front—*la chica bonita* had supreme skills in the bedroom. But by far, the one thing about her that made me shiver was the fact that she was feeling just as strongly for me. She showed it by doing little things that let me know I was always on her mind—little love notes hidden for me to find, phone calls during the day just to say hi, special gifts for no reason at all.

"Just because you're my *papi, chulo.*"

A smile always crept onto my face when I thought about Mariana. So basically, I was always smiling. I was lucky to have found her. And on Valentine's Day, I let her know just how special she was to me. I slaved in the kitchen and cooked steamed rice with broccoli and corn, baked chicken that my mother would love, and topped it off with Mariana's favorite desert—homemade apple pie. Well, at least that's what they said at the bakery.

As we ate the five-star meal over candlelight, soft jazz played in the background. I watched Mariana as she ate. I loved to see the way her two-toned lips closed over the fork. I loved to watch her chew. Everything she did screamed sex appeal to me. When we had finished eating, we held each other in a tight embrace and rocked back and forth slowly to the sounds of Norman Brown. With my lips resting at the side of her head, I said, "I love you."

Mariana looked up at me. "I love you too."

I squeezed her petite frame and kissed her forehead.

Hearing her saying that and seeing the sincerity in her eyes made me really appreciate life and all the things we go through. Had I never gone through all of the shit with Danita, I would have never found Mariana.

"I'm a lucky man," I said softly.

Mariana smiled. "Yes you are."

We made love that night.

Slow love.

The kind that lovers make when everything is right and nothing could ever be wrong.

The next morning, as Mariana snuggled against me, with her leg draped over mine, I stared up at the ceiling and exhaled away frustration and pain. I was in love again—only this time it truly felt real. As Mariana brought her body closer to mine, I kissed her forehead and inhaled the raspberry scent of her hair. I couldn't imagine anything else being more right.

24

Stephen

It was almost impossible to believe that I'd once been on the verge of doing what I was about to do with the wrong woman. The person I'd been, the life I'd had, seemed unreal. Almost as though it had never happened.

Life was good. The best it had ever been. And I just knew deep down that it was only going to get better.

That's why standing outside of Mariana's place with a diamond ring in my hand felt so right. She was the one for me.

Before driving over to pop the question, I called my parents' house to tell them that I was going to propose. My pops was the only person home at the time, which was cool with me, because he was really the person I wanted to talk to.

"Pops, do you remember me telling you about Mariana?"

"The Latin girl you said you've been dating?

Yeah, as much as you've spoken about her, I feel like I know her already. You like her a lot, don't you?"

"Pops, I love her. I know that not a lot of time has passed since I've met her, but I know in my heart that it's right between us. I feel complete when she's with me. I know I thought I felt that way about Danita, but with Mariana it's different. I truly do love her. And I believe—no, I know—she feels the same way about me."

"You may or not agree with this, but I want to marry Mariana, Pops. She's the one. I know it. I just wanted to let you know what I intended to do. I didn't say this then, but the talk we had back in November meant a lot to me. Until that talk, I was planning on closing myself up and never letting anyone get inside of me again. But you convinced me not to. What you said hit me, Pops. Hit me hard. It was because of your words that I fell in love with Mariana."

"I didn't say anything special, son."

"No, Pops, you did. You told me to love and give all of myself. That's the only way to do it, remember?"

My father smiled the very smile I had inherited from him. "I remember."

"Well, I did just that with Mariana. I didn't hold back. And now I am happier than I've ever been. I want to ask her to marry me. I don't need any more time to pass to know that this is the right thing to do."

My father was silent for a few seconds, which made me wonder if he didn't like my decision. Not that it would have really mattered, because I was still going to go through with it, but still, I was hoping to get his blessing.

"I first saw your mother at a party your Uncle Myles threw way back in the day," he finally said. "He was always throwing parties back then. If a happening party was going down, you could be sure your uncle had been the promoter-slash-host. I was about your age; well, maybe a little younger—twenty-six, actually—and working for Bulova watch company in their customer service department. I was never really a party animal, so that night I had planned to camp out in front of the TV and just relax. I only ended up going to the party because your uncle called me and begged me to go. He had more people than he had anticipated coming, and he needed my help to make sure things stayed calm."

I remained silent, but nodded my head. Although in his fifties, my father was still a burly man. I could see him keeping the peace back in his day.

"I was breaking up a scuffle between two drunken fools when your mother walked in with her girlfriends. I had to pick my jaw up from the ground, she was that attractive. You get your looks from her. Anyway, for the rest of the night, I forgot all about keeping the peace. The only thing I could do was stare at your mother. I watched her that whole night. Watched her talk to her friends, watched her dance, watched her laugh, and then I watched her leave. I never got up the nerve to approach her.

"I didn't see her again until almost two months later at another party Myles was throwing. Ever since that first night I'd seen your mother, I'd become a partying fool. I went to every party I could, just hoping to see her again. Only I promised my-self that I wouldn't let the night end without ask-ing her for her name and number."

"How did you know she didn't have a boyfriend?"

"Oh, I checked. I did some extensive research on your mother after I had first laid eyes on her. So, I knew the road was clear for me. That night, when I finally saw her again, I did what I said I would. I walked right up to her with my chest out and my head held high. I was determined to know her." He paused and sighed.

I chuckled at the excitement in his voice. I closed my eyes and leaned back in my sofa. I could see my pops as a young and handsome version of Billy Dee Williams with muscles, approaching my mother, a knockout as Jayne Kennedy.

You go, Pops.

"So, what happened?"

I couldn't see him, but I could tell he had been smiling when he said, "We got married three months later."

I laughed. "Wow."

"I'm happy for you, son. Really happy."

"Thanks, Pops. I'm happy for me too!"

"I have to ask you one thing, though."

"Shoot."

"Does she know about Danita?"

"No. I haven't told her about her."

"Tell her, son. Before you get married. Let her know how much you loved Danita and how bad she hurt you. Then let Mariana know how she changed your life. Let her know how important she is to you."

"I will, Pops."

"Good boy. Son, if you know Mariana's the one, then time doesn't matter."

"Thanks again, Pops."

Standing outside of Mariana's door, I was never more sure about anything. I knocked. When Mariana opened the door, her smile and squeal reassured me that I'd made the right choice.

"Papi chulo!" She threw her arms around me and kissed me on my lips, forehead, and nose. "What are you doing here?"

"I was going through withdrawal and had to come and see you?"

She gave me a sexy smile. "Is that right?"

I kissed her passionately. "Absolutely. So can I come in?"

"Hmm . . . I guess it wouldn't be a good idea for me jump your bones out here."

"Jump my bones, huh?" I walked in and closed the door. "Is that what you plan on doing?"

"And then some," she whispered.

We made love right there in her living room, never stopping until we were both satisfied. After we were finished, and had somehow found a way to make it to the bedroom, we lay naked in each other's arms. The blinds were left open, so the room was dark, save for the rays of moonlight coming in through the window.

"I love you, Mariana," I whispered, caressing her arms.

"I love you too, *papi.*"

"I have a question for you."

"What's that?"

"Is forever a long time?"

"Forever is forever," she replied. "It's only a long time if you're with the wrong person. If you're with the right person, it's not long enough."

"That's what I wanted to hear." I kissed her forehead and then removed the ring box from under my pillow. I slipped my hand under her chin and lifted her face, so that her eyes met mine.

I presented the box with an open palm. "Forever doesn't even come close to being long enough with you. I would need a thousand forevers."

I opened the box and took a deep breath. The ring dazzled in the glow of the moonlight. "Mariana," I said slowly, "You came into my life when I needed you the most. You have changed it in ways that you don't even know about. You are everything to me, and I never want to be without you. I want forever to go on and on, with no end in sight. Mariana . . . will you marry me?"

I held my breath as she stared at me through teary eyes. She didn't move, didn't speak, and almost looked like she didn't breathe. She just watched me and let tears streak down across her cheeks. She didn't even attempt to wipe them away. I wasn't sure what she was thinking, and I suddenly got nervous. Had I been wrong to do this now? Did she really love me the way she'd said she had? I held the ring and took deep breaths.

Finally, as I was really starting to lose hope, Mariana woke from her trance and planted her lips on mine. When she pulled away, she took the ring, slipped it on, and looked at me.

"I would've married you after the first week we met."

* * *

Carlos looked at me through the mirror as he straightened his bow tie. "You ready for this, bro? You ready to step out of the game?"

"Kid, I'm ready."

"Aight bro, I'ma miss your ass running with me. But I know how happy you are, so it's all good."

"Thanks, man."

"Besides, I may not be in the game for too long either."

I looked at Carlos. "Word?"

"Yeah, man. Tianna's no joke. I'm starting to feel like I may not be in the game too much longer either."

"Damn! My boy has finally been bitten. That's good to hear, man."

"Yeah well, just don't spread the word around too much. You know I have my rep to keep up. I don't want to break the other females' hearts just yet."

"But they will be breaking, right?" I asked, giving him a don't-screw-up-a-good-thing look.

"No doubt. But anyway . . . enough about me. This is your day, bro. Damn, I can't believe you're getting married. I mean, shit, after everything you went through with Danita, this is the last thing I would've expected. You proposed to her what, three months after you met?"

"Two. And yeah, I had never really expected to be falling in love. But man, we were meant to be together. Shit, truth be told, Danita brought us together. If she wouldn't have done what she did, I would've never moved, and I would never have met Mariana."

"Yeah, I guess that's true. Actually, Danita did right by all of us while she was doing her dirt."

I nodded. What he said was true. He moved to Jacksonville and took a job as an art teacher for one of the high schools. He still continued counseling troubled kids, his true passion, only in Jacksonville now.

He made the move after coming down to visit me for the third time. The sun, the warmth, and the women had gotten to him. He applied for teaching positions while visiting, and when the offer was made to him, he didn't hesitate to take it. He met Tianna Wilkins at the school. She's the algebra teacher there. Her sharp wit and no-nonsense personality is a perfect match for his sense of humor and lightheartedness.

"Maybe we should send Danita a present, huh?" I said.

"Yeah, let's send her a wedding picture." Carlos laughed and turned toward me. "Man, it's almost hard to believe that all happened a year ago already."

"Yeah," I said, tying my leather shoes and slipping into my jacket. "Time flies when you're having fun."

"You ever talk to her?"

I shook my head. "I was done with her the night I kicked my man's ass."

"Wish I could have seen that, bro," Carlos said with a laugh. "You ever think about her?"

"Every once in a while. I mean, I may see something that reminds me of her, and she'll cross my mind. But I'll be honest, man, I'm so happy with Mariana that as quickly as Danita crosses my mind, she's gone just as fast. Mariana just makes me whole. She's the one I've been looking for my whole life."

Carlos stood beside me. He had his jacket on also. "That's good, bro. I know you guys are going to last. You guys belong together, that's for sure. I know you'll give her all of you, and she's going to do the same for you. She loves you. I can see it when she looks at you."

"Yeah, I think she does too."

"So, marriage, huh? Just think, in another hour, you are officially off the market. Again, I ask you, you ready?"

"Been ready."

"Just making sure your mind hasn't changed."

"Impossible."

"Good."

"Hey man, listen, before I do this, I just wanted to thank you for always being there for me. I may not have been here if wasn't for you trying to keep me straight. I appreciate it, man. And I love you."

"Bros for life, kid."

I gave my best man a pound and a hug. Then, my father and brother walked into the room. They too were dressed in their black tuxes with baby blue bow ties. Being the man of the hour, I had on a black bow tie.

My pops smiled and walked up to me. He was looking damn sharp. "How are you holding up, son?"

"I'm cool, Pops. I'm ready."

"Well, at least *you're* ready," Kyle said, looking as equally sharp in his tux. "Because the women sure as hell aren't, and the guests are getting antsy."

"Well, I guess we had better calm them down," Carlos said.

"You guys go ahead. I just want a quick minute alone."

When they left the room, I turned and faced a crucifix of Jesus Christ hanging above the priest's desk. Looking at it, I whispered, "I know I'm not the most religious guy out here, but I wanted to thank you for answering my prayers. You may not have answered them as quickly as I would've liked or in the way that I had wanted you to, but you were always listening."

I left the room and got married.

Mariana and I went to Aruba for our honeymoon. While there, we enjoyed all of the sights, sounds, and tastes that the Caribbean island had to offer. We went snorkeling in the shallow waters of Malmok Beach, went swimming and relaxed in the white powder sand of Palm Beach, took horseback-riding tours, and explored the island's hilly terrain. At night, we went to the action-filled casinos and a few of the other clubs, where we danced until our feet hurt. We took full advantage of our time together. When we weren't going out, we'd stay in the hotel and go to some of the beach barbecues or cocktail parties the hotel threw. We also enjoyed the hotel's fashion shows, local dance groups, limbo and fire dances, and sounds of the steel bands.

When we wanted a more sedate pace, we would just enjoy a tropical drink on a moonlit patio, under a star-filled sky, or a romantic stroll on the beach. And when we weren't doing any of those things, we'd make love. We made love in the morning when we woke up, during the afternoon when we'd take a break, and at night before we passed out. With each moment of passion, we reaffirmed the love we had vowed for each another.

The honeymoon, paid for by my pops and her father, who had hit it off immediately at the wedding, was a trip neither one of us would forget.

Even though we hated leaving the island paradise, we were both looking forward to going back home and lying together as man and wife in our own bed. We had bought a town house together after we had become engaged. We wanted a new place to call our own. We chose a town house with three bedrooms—to accommodate the family that we planned to have.

After collecting our mail and saying hello to our neighbors, who all wanted to know about our trip, we escaped into the sanctuary of our home. Upon walking in, we heard the beeping of the answering machine. Mariana and I looked at each other and smiled—it was back to reality.

I kissed my wife on the lips. "I'll check the two thousand messages."

"And I'll be waiting for you in the shower."

"In that case, I'll check them later."

"No, you go and check them now, *papi*. I need to get the bathroom ready."

I looked at Mariana with puppy-dog eyes and pouted my bottom lip playfully. She laughed. "Go check them, *chulo*. It'll be worth it when you come in."

That, and a seductive smile and batting eyelashes sent a tingle up my spine. I nodded and hurried to the machine. As Mariana went into the bathroom and closed and locked the door, I hit play. The first few messages were the ones I had expected we'd receive. Everyone wanting to know how the trip had been. What we did. If we'd started a family while we were there. Call us when you get in. Yada, yada, yada. I listened halfheartedly to most of the messages, until I heard Carlos's voice. An immediate smile formed on my face. I'd missed my dog. But as the message played, my smile quickly went away. When it was finished, I played it again to see if what I'd heard had been for real.

Yo . . . This is Carlos. Ummm . . . somethin' bad has happened, bro. Ummm . . . I just figured I should call and tell you. Ummm . . . it's about Danita. She . . . uh . . . she's in the hospital. I've heard that she may not make it. She was in a bad car accident. Call me when you get back . . .

I stood silent for a long while, digesting what I'd heard. The message was almost a week old.

I couldn't move. Danita had been in an accident. She may not make it. Chills ran along my spine. My heartbeat tripled. My legs felt like rubber. I went to the couch and sat down.

Danita may not make it.

The statement didn't seem real to me. Didn't seem possible.

My eyes welled. I didn't try to wipe my tears away as they fell.

I turned and faced the bathroom, where Mariana had the water running and was waiting for me. As my pops had suggested, I told her all about

Danita before we got married. She had no problem with my past because it had been just that. Hopefully she wouldn't have a problem with my needing to go back to Maryland one last time.

25

Danita

I was silent as I watched myself lying unconscious in the hospital bed. I had an IV in my arm, a breathing mask over my face. My eyes were swollen shut, my lip stitched up and swollen as well, numerous scratches on my forehead and cheeks. I looked terrible. Had I not been in the coma I was in, I'm sure I would have felt worse. But as it was, unconscious and barely holding on, I couldn't feel a thing.

I watched my mama, who sat beside me with tears streaking from her eyes. She held my hand in hers tightly, refusing to let go. She hadn't slept in days. She couldn't sleep. Could barely even eat. The only thing she could do was hold onto my hand, touch my forehead, and beg me to wake up. Beg me to hold on and not let go.

I wanted to listen to her. I wanted with all my might to open my eyes and tell her that everything was going to be okay. That I was going to make it.

But I couldn't.

The accident had been bad. It had been night-time, and I had collided head-on into a tree while taking a back road. It was raining, pouring actually. A mini-monsoon. Puddles lined the roads. The driving lines were barely visible.

The day of my accident had been the day of Stephen's wedding.

I'd found out that he was getting married from Latrice, who'd found out from someone on the job that Stephen had occasionally spoken to. The news of his coming nuptials had been devastating for me. Despite everything that had happened and the fact that we hadn't spoken in over a year, I still held out the hope that, somehow, he and I were going to find our way back to each other's arms. I saw our being together as destiny, and felt in my soul that everything between us had happened only to help make us stronger. Especially myself.

Before the mistakes, I was weak. I lived with my past sitting on my shoulders, constantly talking to me, telling me that my future could never be any different. That, no matter where I went, it was always going to be with me. That the men in my life were always going to be the same because I would make it so. Losing Stephen really helped me realize that if I didn't learn to let bad memories go, my past was going to be right. That I would never truly be able to be happy.

It wasn't easy, but I eventually learned to let all of the hurt and pain I'd been through become just a memory, and not something that would rule my life. I learned to accept that not all men were the same. With each passing day, I climbed up out of the cave I'd been dwelling in and grew stronger and more determined to never look backward. I didn't know when our reunion would happen, but I was just certain that Stephen and I would come together again, and when we did, with my new-found strength, we were going to live a beautiful life together.

I began making strides. I was doing better in my personal life. I'd quit the law firm, closing the door on that dark chapter in my life, and gone back to the Limited at the mall, and within a matter of months became manager. I wasn't looking for anything serious, because again I knew it was only going to be a matter of time for Stephen and me, but I began to date occasionally. I was moving on, but holding onto the destiny at the same time. But then I heard about the wedding.

The day of the accident had been a miserable one for me. I couldn't focus and I felt sick all day long. I never knew the date of the wedding, but I just knew in my soul that on that particular day I was losing Stephen for good.

I went out in the rain because I didn't want to be alone in the house. I didn't want to hear the echoes of Stephen's voice saying "I do" to some-one else. I'd been hearing them since Latrice broke the news to me. In my dreams, in the air around me.

I do.

I do.

I didn't have a destination that evening. I just wanted to drive. I didn't care about the downpour. Sadness, frustration, and anger bombarded me like the pellets of rain hitting the car. I didn't in-tentionally go out there to get into an accident, but as the thunder exploded and lightning bright-ened the sky, exposing the deer standing in the middle of a back road I'd been on, for a brief moment I thought of doing just that. But it had only been a fleeting moment. Unfortunately when the moment passed and I made a move to veer to the left to avoid hitting the deer, I hit a deep puddle and ended up hydroplaning. I tried to get control of the car, but my natural instinct caused me to slam on my brakes. I barreled head-on into the tree after that. Somehow I didn't die upon impact, although, as I stared down at myself, I knew that the Reaper was coming.

My mama prayed to God and begged me to wake up again. I opened my mouth to speak to her, to tell her how much I loved her, but there were no sounds with my words. My mama cried. Touched my forehead again. Squeezed my hand. Told me how precious I was to her and how much she loved me. I should have let go at that particular moment. I should have moved on. But I didn't.

And I knew why.

26

Stephen

Latrice met Mariana and me at the hospital. I introduced my wife and then asked the only question I could: "How is she?"

Latrice looked at me and shook her head. I hadn't seen her since I had told her I was leaving E-Systems. She looked like she hadn't slept in days. Black circles sat heavily beneath her eyes. Her hair was disheveled and her clothing was wrinkled.

"How did this happen?" I asked.

After I listened to Carlos's message, I called him back at home and on his cell but didn't get him. I left a message and then told Mariana that I needed to go to Maryland and why. As beautiful as she was understanding, she had no problem with my need to go and offered to go with me for support. I was glad for her company.

Three hours after arriving home, we were back on the plane. Before we took off, I tried Danita's mother, and when I couldn't reach her I called Latrice's cell. When she answered, I told her that we were coming and asked if she could meet us at the hospital. I told her not to give me the details until I'd gotten there because I didn't want to be any more of a wreck than I already was. I needed to be strong.

When we arrived at Howard County Hospital, I could barely breathe. The former love of my life was about to die. The thought constricted my lungs and made my muscles tight. My palms were sweaty as I held Mariana's hand in mine.

She kissed me before we walked inside, then looked at me and smiled. "I have you," she said with a reassuring smile, "but she needs you right now." Her eyes were glistening with tears.

I kissed her and then we went inside.

"She crashed into a tree. It was pouring rain. She shouldn't have been out." Tears leaked from Latrice's eyes and cascaded down across her round cheeks.

"When?"

"Last Saturday night."

My wedding day.

I shivered. "She's been in a coma for that long?"

Latrice nodded.

"And she hasn't come out of it at all?"

"No. The doctors are amazed that she's held on this long."

"Damn," I whispered. "How's her mother? Is she okay?"

"Ms. Sheila is in there with her. She's been here for the entire week."

"Damn," I whispered again. "Are we allowed to see her?"

Latrice wiped her eyes and said softly, "I'll take you."

I looked again at Mariana. "I'll be back."

As I walked beside Latrice, thoughts of disbelief swam through my head. I couldn't believe that this had really happened. When we got to the room, Latrice put her hand on my shoulder. "Stephen, before you go in there, I just want you to know something."

I looked at Latrice, who had a steady flow of tears coming from her swollen eyes.

I had my own stream of tears flowing. "Yeah?"

"I think the only reason she's holding on is because of you."

I looked at Latrice and nodded and then I walked into the room. As I stepped in, the sight of Danita's mother sitting beside her daughter's bed, reading scriptures softly from a Bible, greeted me. She looked up at me and then rose from her chair. I kept my back close to the door. I couldn't seem to make my feet move. The room was dark, except for the light that her mother was using. Sounds of the EKG monitor reverberated loudly in the air.

"Thank you for coming," her mother said, wrapping her arms around me.

"I just found out today," I said my throat constricted. "Had I found out sooner . . ."

"I know, baby. I know."

She grabbed my hand and looked toward her daughter. "I can't believe I'm going to lose my baby."

"I'm sorry, Ms. Evans," I said, wiping tears away. "I'm so sorry."

"She's special, you know. So very special."

"Yes, she is."

"She loved you, Stephen. Loved you with all her heart."

"I know."

"You were good to her, Stephen. I'll always be thankful for that. I'll always be thankful for you. Go over there and say good-bye to my child. I think the Lord is coming soon."

I nodded and exhaled my words. "Yes, ma'am."

Ms. Evans gave my hand a squeeze and then took her Bible and walked out of the room.

Left alone, I stood stock-still and listened to the silence in the room, interrupted only by the beeping of Danita's heartbeat. Somehow, I managed to make my feet move, and took slow steps toward the bed.

"Danita," I whispered. I reached out my hand and lightly touched her bandaged forehead. The hairs on my arms and the back of my neck rose. I lowered my head and sighed.

"Danita," I whispered, barely able to find my voice. "Danita, I'm here. It's me. It's Stephen."

I paused and watched her. I watched for any subtle movement: a twitch in her finger, a batting of an eyelash. But I saw nothing. I caressed her forehead again and then took her hand in mine. I watched her breathing mask rhythmically fill with steam as she breathed.

"Please, Danita," I said. "Wake up. We need you. Don't leave. Can you hear me? I'm here for you, okay? Open your eyes for me. Squeeze my hand."

I clenched my jaws and kept my eyes focused on hers and continued to look for any sign of movement. As I did, images of Danita from the past flashed through my mind. I could see her smile when she was happy, see her frown when she was sad. Her eyes sparkled in my head. "Please wake up, Danita. You're not supposed to be here."

A river of tears ran down my cheeks now. "Open your eyes for me, lady. Just a fraction."

As my tears fell from my chin to the bed, Danita remained unmoving and unresponsive. I inhaled and exhaled and wiped my tears away. But even as I did that, a new wave fell harder. I bit down on my bottom lip and listened to the heart monitor beeping. Its sound was noisy and brought a chill to my bones.

For the next hour I spoke to her. I spoke about old times and all of the things we used to do together. I spoke about trips we'd taken, movies we'd seen—anything. I laughed as I spoke to her. I cried as I reminisced. I spoke of all the good times, which had far outweighed the bad. I spoke about the love we had shared for each another, and the love I still had in my heart for her. I went on and on, until I had nothing else to say.

Then I removed her breathing mask. "I will always love you," I said quietly. I bent over and gave her a soft, gentle kiss on her lips. "Good-bye, Danita."

I took one last look at Danita Evans, and then turned to leave. Before I reached the door, the rhythmic beeping became one long flat line. I walked out of the room and let the door whisper shut behind me.

When I had reached the waiting area, Mariana was sitting quietly beside Ms. Evans. Latrice looked at me from her seat. "She's gone," I said solemnly.

Latrice broke down and had to be consoled by Mariana. I stood somber, with tears coming from my own eyes. Ms. Evans stood up and approached me. Amazingly enough, her eyes were dry. She enveloped me in a hug again. "My baby is at peace now. Thank you for bringing her happiness one last time."

I held onto her for a few seconds and then let go. She had a smile on her face. Without saying a word to anyone else, I reached out my hand for Mariana. She rose from her chair and came toward me and opened her arms for me to fall into.

"Thank you for coming," I whispered as she softly rubbed my back.

She kissed me on my head and said, "I love you."

"I love you back," I whispered.

I said good-bye to Latrice and Ms. Evans and then took Mariana's hand and walked away from my past. But as we neared the exit doors, I saw something to my right that made me pause. Looking toward the hallway leading to Danita's room, I saw him. He was leaning against the wall outside of her door. His face was in his hands, and his shoulders were slumped. I stood and watched him for a long minute, until Mariana tugged on my hand.

"Do you know him?"

I kept my eyes focused on him as he cried. "I know him," I said simply.

"Do you want to go and talk to him? I can wait, baby."

"No," I said with an exhale. "There's nothing to say."

Danita had waited for me.

EPILOGUE

Diary,

Stephen is getting married today. It is over. There is no chance now. My heart is broken. I lost him because I didn't love him the way I should have. I can only hope that whoever he has found loves him in the way he deserves. He's one-of-a-kind, and I will never forget him or the love he gave to me. He is forever embedded in my heart.

To the woman that has his heart . . . take care of him. Be good to him. He will love you unconditionally. He will always be there to protect you and stand by you. He will never hold back on loving you. Stephen, forgive me for all that I did. And please know that I love you and always will.

Book Club Questions

1. What would your reaction have been after finding a condom in your boyfriend/husband's pocket?

2. Was Stephen's explanation sufficient and did he do enough to ease Danita's mind?

3. Why was Danita so reluctant to let her past go?

4. Do you think Jeff really cared for Danita?

5. Why do you think Danita gave in to Jeff? Was she truly in love with him?

6. Would you have had the same reaction as Latrice upon finding out about that your best friend was sleeping with her boss?

7. Explain the friendship Danita's indiscretions?

8. Do you think Danita truly understood how bad she'd hurt Stephen?

9. Was Stephen wrong for attacking Jeff?

10. In Mariana, Stephen found a love that he'd been looking for. Had he ever really had that with Danita? Or do you think that they would have eventually had problems?

Want some more from Dwayne Joseph?

Read some pages from his new book,

Home Wrecker

Wreaking havoc in stores September 2008

1

Lisette

I'm a home wrecker.
I tear families apart with seduction. A subtle smile somewhere halfway in between innocence and raw sex.

Home wrecker.

C-cup breasts. Twenty-five-inch sized waist. An ass that Beyoncé would envy. That's what I use to lure men away.

Call me the pied piper. Or better yet, the pied pipestress.

Home wrecker.

I'm good at what I do.

I'm not a whore. I'm not a woman desperate for affection. I'm not a friend with benefits. I'm not a mistress.

Breaking up marriages is my profession.

Wives pay me to set up their husbands. Pay good money. Thousands for a few hours of my time. That's about how long it takes me to get a man to forget about the ring on his finger and say to hell with the vows he'd made. A few hours and then he's lost it all. In most cases it's his money, his home, his car, his family. In other cases, it's his manhood. And I don't mean that he becomes John Wayne Bobbitt's distant cousin.

Most women have their men set up because they're tired of being disrespected. They spend their days and nights catering to their men. Cooking, cleaning, taking care of the kids, sexing when it's required. They do all of this yet they're constantly having to deal with lies, deceit, physical and emotional abuse. They suffer day after day, wondering why a man they gave their all to would hurt them the way they do. They suffer until they can't take it anymore.

Then they call me.

They want the son of a bitch trapped. Caught on tape. They want pictures. Sometimes they want to be in the room, watching, getting a firsthand view of the man doing what most of them knew he'd do. Of course, some still hold out hope that their man would change his mind at the last minute because he loves his wife just too much to betray her. But that never happens, because I don't allow it to happen. In the end, the bastard's caught and papers are served.

Game over.

That's when a man loses it all.

They lose their manhood, however, when their women have them set up strictly for power and control. These women never have any intention of divorcing their men. See, instead of presenting the evidence and taking half, they hold that evidence over their men's heads. Whatever they want they get. Whenever they want it, it's theirs. No complaints about how much the piece of jewelry or a new pair of shoes cost. No put-downs. No mouth at all, because while their men are doing or spending whatever it takes to keep from having to give up their house or car, or to avoid shelling out thousands in child support (millions in some cases), the women get free rein to go and fuck the pool boy, the gardener, or the sexy gym instructor with the tight ass.

Flip the coin and the side's the same. Either way you look at it, my services provide financial stability. Most of all, I give back what most of my clients should have never lost.

Control.

Some prefer the other option, but for a lot of woman—at least the ones that deal with me, replacing that is better than getting half any day.

Past

2

Setting up men for a living was never in my career plan, but when I look back on my past, it's obvious that I was always headed down that road.

See, at thirteen years old I understood I had power over men.

Equipped with a thirteen-year-old's curvaceous and fully developed body, I realized back then that all it took to get what I wanted was a subtle, seductive smile, a sexy gaze, or a you-know-you-want-it stance.

My father was the first man I'd learned to control.

Most people assumed I'd had him wrapped around my finger because he loved me unconditionally. I was his daughter, his princess, but I knew better. My father was a pervert, who was always taking side glances at me and looking me up and down. He used to love to accidentally walk in on me when I was showering or getting undressed. But instead of excusing himself and leaving right away, he would take long, lingering seconds to admire "how grown" his little girl was. He never touched me improperly, but I could see in his eyes that he wanted to fuck me good.

I should have been uncomfortable and disgusted by the fact that my own father had sexual thoughts about me, but I never was. I was amused, actually. I mean, there I was, a thirteen-year-old girl getting a rise out of a grown man—hell, my own father!

Toying with him, I learned the art of seduction and garnered a true understanding of the type of power I possessed then. With an inviting look, a seductive smile, a sexy stance, I realized I could get whatever I wanted.

Through my father, I understood just how weak men were. I learned that if you teased them just enough, their imaginations would run wild, their dicks would swell, and they'd become puppets doing whatever it was you wanted them to.

My mother saw the power I had over my father and tried time and time again to stand in my way. But although I was young, I'd been too in tune with my sex appeal, and by the time I was fifteen, she left my father and me. She never admitted it, but I think she was jealous of the fact that, up until his fatal heart attack, I could have still manipulated the hell out him.

Manipulation.

Break it down.

A woman must have come up with the word.

I continued to learn and love the power of manipulation through my teenage years and on into my early twenties. There was just nothing as intense to me as pulling a man's strings to get what I wanted without having to give up anything in return. And that was always the case. Boys and men bought me things, took me places, and did anything I told them to or asked, and unless I wanted it to happen, they never even got a whiff of my pussy.

Manipulation.

Control.

The words were synonymous.

Playing men was always like a game to me, because I never really needed them.

I came to the realization in my early teens that in order for me to truly have control over a man, I had to be independent and successful. A woman that could play a man, but didn't have her own shit, got no respect from me, because in my eyes they were weak-minded. They may have had the tits and ass and knew how to use them, but they lacked intelligence, because if they were truly using their brains, they would realize that a woman who had her own shit was far more desirable.

See, men are simple. They do all of their rationalization with their dicks and think that because God gave them chest hair, they're supposed be the dominant one.

A woman that needs nothing is a woman most wanted because they're viewed as a challenge. Bring your own car into the relationship—a man will want to buy you a better, more expensive one. Have your own home—a man will want you to move into his. Have your own money and he'll say to hell with the price and empty out his own wallet.

Men are driven by the need to impress. Women who understand this are the ones that get the most respect from me.

My mother, as beautiful as she was, never brought anything to the table, which is why my father never truly respected her. She always used to complain about how I was just like my father. I guess she's been right, because I didn't have much respect for her either. To this day, we still don't have much of a relationship.

Like I said, I never intended on becoming a home wrecker.

Prior to my career change I was the head buyer for LeVor Fashions—an up-and-coming urban fashion company that was bringing some serious heat to the powerhouses like Sean John and Rocawear. On a day-to-day basis I met with established designers as well as new, fresh designers and basically said yea or nay to the ideas they'd come up with. LeVor was doing great before I'd gotten there, but I can't lie—I had a lot to do with the company's growth over a four-year period.

I always had a keen eye when it came to fashion. I just knew what did and didn't look good. What would or wouldn't work. To me, style went hand in hand with the power a woman possessed. It was all part of the package.

During my junior year in college, I was able to land an internship with LeVor, starting out as an assistant for the head buyer at that time. While I did the minute tasks like make copies, put away files, and run errands, my mentor would allow me to get into the thick of things by seeking out my opinion, which actually mattered. Under her, I learned the dos and don'ts of the industry, and I got a true understanding of trends and how to rec ognize what they were and when they would happen.

During my senior year, I was given my first major task of choosing the design to go with a pair of jeans the company was going to kick off their summer line with. The pair I chose was supposed to be the teaser, but it turned out to be their biggest seller for the season. Impressed with everything I'd done during my internship, LeVor hired me on as a junior-level buyer after I graduated.

I did that for three years and enjoyed great success in my role until I was suddenly propelled to head buyer when my mentor quit unexpectedly and went to work for the competition. So there I was at twenty-six, the youngest person in the company, with an executive position. I had a six-figure salary, drove a Mercedes, and owned a luxurious condo overlooking the city. I was a single and successful badass, honey-complected black woman, and the men loved and hated me. They loved me because I had the beauty and the brains. They hated me because I couldn't be tamed.

Remember: Control was what it was all about for me.

Life was good for me back then. Shit, life was great. Especially my career. I was respected. I was envied. I never expected my career to change.

But then I went to Texas.

3

Houston, Texas.
Sofitel Hotel.

At the bar in the lounge, sitting with the VP of marketing, Marlene Stewart.

That was where my career changed.

We were having drinks. Me, a cosmopolitan. Marlene—white wine. We were in Houston attending the fashion show of one of the country's hottest female rappers—XXXstacy. Like P. Diddy, Jay-Z, and other rappers with huge followings, XXXstacy decided to expand her tiny empire and step into the world of fashion. She didn't design shit, but with her name, XXXstacy Wear was destined to blow up.

Some top people at LeVor received insider information about XXXstacy's desire to get into fashion, and with relentless pursuit, the company managed to work out a deal with her that would be beneficial to both sides.

Houston was XXXstacy's hometown, so it was naturally the site for the premier showing. I'd designed some and approved many of what the public was going to see. Marlene had been responsible for the buzz. Countless hours put in, XXXstacy Wear was more our baby than XXXstacy's herself. After one-too-many last-minute meetings, we were in the lounge winding down before the big showing the next day.

Marlene was an attractive, older, white female in her mid-forties who could have easily passed for being in her mid-thirties. She was an obsessive woman. Obsessive about her work. Obsessive about her body. Obsessive about her husband.

"Fucking asshole." Marlene snapped her cell phone shut.

I looked at her, but didn't say anything. That had been the fifth time in the past seven minutes that she'd done that. I took a sip of my cosmo and waited for her to curse again.

"Fucking asshole. He's probably fucking her right now." Marlene angrily passed her hand through her shoulder-length brown hair.

I took another sip of my drink, blotted the corner of my mouth with my thumb and index finger, and said, "Why don't you just divorce him?"

Marlene frowned. "And deal with the scrutiny from friends and family? No thank you."

"But he's fucking his secretary."

As I said that, a man sitting on the stool beside Marlene looked in our direction. With my eyes I told him to mind his business. He got up and left.

Marlene sipped her wine and gave an irritated smile. "Yes he is. Unfortunately, I've never been able to prove that."

"No e-mails? No text messages?"

"No secret love notes. Nothing."

"So how do you know for certain that he's fucking her?"

Marlene gave me a come-on-now look. "You know as a woman we just know. Besides, I can smell her pussy on him whenever he's been with her. It's kind of tart, like maybe she only cleans it once a day."

I wrinkled my nose. "That's nasty."

"She's nasty. The skinny bitch. Smiling in my face whenever I see her, as if she's really pulling something over on me. Pathetic."

"Maybe she's smiling because she knows you know," I said, raising my eyebrows.

"Then she's a skinny, pathetic, arrogant bitch for thinking her inexperienced pussy is that good."

I took a sip of cosmo again and nodded. "Inexperienced or not, Marlene, it must be something to have your husband swimming in it."

Marlene looked at me. My honesty had stung. She flipped open her cell again.

"Why are you calling him?"

Marlene hit the talk button to send the call. "I don't know," she said, her voice filled with frustration.

I frowned. Shook my head. I never understood why women did that. Stressed over a man.

"Fucking asshole." Marlene slammed her phone down on the bar counter.

"Why did you marry him, Marlene?"

"You've seen him. Thirty, a face as pretty as Brad Pitt, a body as delicious as the Rock's."

"So he's attractive. That can't be the only reason you married him."

Marlene looked at me, then down at her phone and sighed. "He can fuck."

"What?"

"I said, he can fuck."

I spit out a little of the cosmo I'd been drinking at the time and laughed. "Are you serious? That's why you married him?"

Marlene passed her hand through her hair again. Something she did when she was aggravated. "I've been married twice before, Lisette, to men who were my age and were on my level, both mentally and financially. They were nice, decent men. Good conversationalist. Driven. Had good credit. Pretty much what you'd want in a man."

I shrugged my shoulders. "So what was the problem?"

"For all of the good qualities they had, there was one problem. A major problem."

"Let me guess . . . they couldn't fuck."

"They had dicks, but had no clue about how to use them."

I couldn't help but laugh.

"I'm serious, Lisette! They were so unfamiliar with their own tool, that I spent too many damn nights taking care of myself after they were supposed to. It was frustrating. Eventually I got tired of fucking myself and started fucking other men. My first husband caught me cheating. That's why the marriage ended. I divorced my second husband before he could catch me."

I laughed again, finished off my cosmo, and cued the bartender with my index finger for another. "So Steve put it on you, huh?"

"Steve fucks like he invented it. I met him at the gym. He used to pursue me daily. At first I used to brush him off. I mean, I'm almost fifty. I couldn't possibly mess with a man fifteen years my junior, right?"

"But you did."

"He was persistent. Always approaching me with his sexy ways, and his sexy pretty-boy smile. Always ready with the compliments. I finally gave in one day, and agreed to go out with him to dinner. I figured what was the harm. It was just dinner."

"I'm guessing it turned into a long dinner and an early breakfast."

Marlene closed her eyes briefly. I could tell that she was reminiscing. "Lisette," she said, opening them, "I didn't plan on sleeping with him that night, but with the alcohol, his looks, and the fact that it had been months since I'd had any, we ended up going back to my place."

"And you were ready to marry him the next day, right?"

Marlene finished her wine, did the same finger motion to the bartender, and said, "Trust me . . . if you fucked Steve, you'd be hooked too."

I closed my eyes a bit. "I doubt that."

"Steve's good, honey. Damn good."

"And now the secretary is getting some."

"Yes. The bitch."

"And instead of having to hear any crap about being divorced for a third time, you're calling him practically every five minutes?"

Closing her cell again, Marlene said, "Yes. I don't need to hear the shit from anyone. I don't want to deal with the judgmental stares. Of all of my friends and family, I'm the one who can't keep a man."

"Have you tried catching him in the act?"

"Of course. Surprise visits to his office. I've come home a day or days early from business trips."

"And you've never caught him?"

"Never."

"But he comes home smelling like tart pussy?"

"Yes."

The bartender brought our drinks and flashed us a smile. He was an attractive brother with an athletic build. Watching his muscles flex, I wondered if he could fuck the way Marlene said Steve could. I stopped wondering when he walked over to a man sitting three bar stools down from us and gave him just too much attention.

Always the good-looking ones.

I looked back at Marlene. She was a mess. Attractive. Fit. Successful. Yet she was irritated and jealous because a man she knew she was too good for, was giving her dick away.

I took a swallow of my fresh cosmo. "Why don't you just set him up?"

"Excuse me?"

"Set him up. Hire a hooker to fuck him."

"I can't do that."

"Why?"

"Because it's wrong."

"You could have been in an accident and that's why you're calling him constantly. Isn't it wrong that he's ignoring your calls?"

Marlene didn't answer.

I continued. "Isn't it wrong that you're emotionally stressed from the fact that the man you married is giving your dick away? The dick that he vowed would only be yours?"

Marlene looked at her phone, whispered, "Fucking asshole."

"Forget a hooker," I said. "A hooker's not good enough. He can pass that off as a mistake. A one-time lapse in judgment. He's human. It wouldn't

happen again. What you need is a friend. A friend
is much worse. She can say he'd been coming on
to her behind your back. She can say that he'd
promised to give her what he gives to you."

"Lisette . . . are you serious?"

"Your friend can say that he'd threatened to flip
the script by telling you that she was the one coming on to him. You wouldn't take her word over his
because he loves you. That's what your friend can
say, came from his mouth."

"Lisette . . ."

"Do you have a friend that would do that?"

"Lisette . . . I . . . I can't."

"Why not?"

"Because."

"Catch him in the act with someone you know,
and your friends and family can't say shit."

"But . . . but . . ."

Marlene paused and fiddled with her glass.

"But what, Marlene? Do you want to continue
being unhappy?"

"No."

"Do you want to continue playing second fiddle
to tart-smelling pussy?"

"No," Marlene said.

"Then set him up. Get someone that you trust."

"But . . . but . . ."

"But what, Marlene?"

"But . . . I don't have any friends that I trust like
that."

Silence overtook our conversation as Marlene
watched me, watching her.

Set him up.

Set him up and no one could say shit.

That's all she had to do to regain control.

I stared at her intensely. Marlene was a good woman. Honest and down-to-earth. Like any other woman, all she wanted was to be loved, respected, and to get some good dick. She didn't deserve Steve's shit.

"I'll do it," I said.

Marlene's eyes widened. "What?"

"I'll do it. I'll set him up."

"You?"

"Yes. He knows me. I've been to your house a few times. He's had opportunities to come on to me.

"But Lisette . . ."

"Do you or do you not want out of this marriage?"

Marlene opened her mouth to protest, but instead dropped her chin to her chest. "Yes," she said.

And there it was.

She wanted out.

I could make it happen.

That's when my career changed.